AN **ELLE ANDERSON** NOVEL

SHADOW
GAME

A. M. ADAIR

STORY MERCHANT BOOKS · LOS ANGELES · 2019

Shadow Game

ISBN-13: 978-1-970157-13-0

Story Merchant Books
400 S. Burnside Avenue, #11B
Los Angeles, CA 90036
www.storymerchantbooks.com

www.529bookdesign.com
Cover: Claire Moore
Interior: Lauren Michelle

Author Facebook: A.M. Adair

For Jake, Arya, and Finn

SHADOW GAME

CHAPTER 1

Elle Anderson was ready to strike. Every muscle was tensed for the attack when her electronic leash ruined the moment. The sound was off but she could still hear it vibrating in her gym bag. *Damnit.* The punch came in from the wrong side; her opponent was a southpaw and she barely blocked the shot. Recovering her focus, she countered the jab with a rapid combination and shot in for the takedown. The impact on the ground was jarring, but Elle had the dominant position and aggressively capitalized on it. Passing her opponent's guard with ease, she sunk in a choke and waited for the inevitable tap.

Standing up, Elle offered her hand. He grudgingly took it.

A voice outside the ring called to her, "This is supposed to be a sparring session, Elle, what the hell was that?"

She looked at the gym manager and shrugged. "Sorry, Scott, figured since he's your young up-and-comer, he could use the challenge." The twenty-something she had just destroyed did not look pleased. Smiling, she told him, "Don't worry, kid. If you don't get your ass kicked now and again, that probably means you're not fighting the right people." Elle knew the real issue; she was a woman, but she pretended not to notice.

Leaving the ring, she dug her cell phone out of her bag. It showed one missed call from a number she recognized. Listening to the voicemail, she heard what sounded like a job offer for a "freelance photographer."

Yes! Time to go to work. She'd just been activated, and someone was going to die. Calling the number in the message, she was given her flight information and location. Grimacing, she told herself not to dwell and just get to work. It was difficult for her to fill the void between jobs—this was her life—but she wouldn't have it any other way. Elle was intelligent, highly skilled in martial arts, an expert marksman, and excelled at ballroom dancing. She checked every box a modern spy could ask for and was psyched her sabbatical was over.

• • •

The second Elle walked off the plane, the sun beat down on her. Sweat ran down the middle of her back and collected along her belt line. She couldn't believe she was back in this damn place. But here she was, in Iraq again.

The country had been beautiful once but, after years of war, it was scarcely recognizable. The moon dust had already started to coat her boots. It was sand so fine it could barely be called sand other than the color. Gravel had been laid on the ground to help keep the stuff from going everywhere each time a gust of wind came through. But it had been a long time since anyone touched it up. Patches where the sand had reclaimed its dominance were everywhere.

She looked around and sighed. *Fucking BIAP.* Baghdad International Airport, it was probably the most built-up base the U.S. Military had in all of Iraq, but since it had been turned over to the Iraqis, things had fallen apart. They could never seem to own up to the responsibilities of taking care of themselves. But that was an easy judgment to make from someone who didn't grow up under the rule of an egomaniacal tyrant who dictated everything about life, including when it was over. Most of the hardened structures around the airfield appeared to still be there, but for some reason it just seemed off to her. She couldn't quite put her finger on it, but it was almost as if the people were simply going through the motions and not really there. Nothing but concrete, sand, and stone everywhere.

She grabbed her bags from the aircrew member pulling them from the cargo area and moved away from the aircraft. As she followed the other passengers toward the hanger, she intentionally lagged behind knowing it would make the guy in the red shirt itchy. There were five other passengers on the C-26, each of them was a Navy SEAL, elite in military circles and lethal. But her instincts had only screamed a warning about him. As the men approached the side door to the hangar, a large, deeply tanned man with black hair slid it open. He squinted from the bright light before putting on dark sunglasses.

Red Shirt turned and looked at her before turning back and sizing up the tan man holding the door. Once Red Shirt was past the man, she called out loud enough for everyone to hear, "Sorry to ask, but is there a restroom nearby?"

The tan man nodded. "The water is jacked up in the one inside. I'll show you where the next closest one is."

Elle followed him behind the hanger to a trailer.

Once inside, he took off the glasses. "It's about damn time, Mama." He smiled and opened his arms.

She dropped her gear and embraced him. He lifted her off the ground in a fierce hug. "You look like shit, Tex, but it's good to see you, too."

He laughed, a deep rumble. Tex was a good man. She considered him one of hers, which meant she knew she could trust him. She tended to be protective of the few she considered hers. "Any issues getting here?" Elle asked.

"We ran behind from the start. Damn Air Force guys didn't want to leave Germany. Can't say I blame them, good beer, better per diem, beautiful women. They kept having engine troubles. I figure they were delaying so they could try and push the flight another day claiming they were too close to crew rest."

He was probably right; all military aircrews played that game from time to time. Their sleep was closely monitored, and the timelines associated with it was not something that could be argued in any case not an emergency. When they hit their time for crew rest, that was it, they were done for a few hours. So, if their timelines could be intentionally varied to allow the aircrew to stay in Germany instead of Iraq, that was a no brainer.

"So how long have you been here?" Elle asked.

"Got here two weeks ago and set up shop. We've got this trailer on loan to facilitate all logistics moves and then another hardened building near a helo pad. We've got it wired with all our comms, computers are up and running, and the monitors are hooked up for watching the ISR feeds. We've been playing nice with the SOF guys, and they've been pretty much leaving us alone since they're doing turnover. We're just one more contractor walking around."

Coming in while the Special Operations Forces or SOF guys were in the middle of turnover, was perfect. SOF guys were the best, but the mission came first for them. So, even if they might be curious about the new faces, as long as her team had the proper security badges and didn't get in the way, they would focus on what needed to be done. Right now, an Army component was turning over with a Navy component. Lots of new faces, lots of moving parts, and enough controlled chaos ensured that no one paid too much attention to her team. By the time things settled down she hoped to be out of there, a couple of weeks, max.

"Where do we stand?"

"Don't you want to get your shit stowed and get settled first?"

She responded with a stare.

"Stupid question, figured. We'll go straight to the war room and I'll bring you up to speed. This building is a little flimsy and exposed, so best not to chat about anything of significance here. There are local national workers that hang around the back side of the hangar to smoke and find shade under the overhang. I've got a truck out in the lot."

Nodding, she went to grab her bag, but Tex beat her to it. She glared at him.

"Just once would you not give me hell for trying to act like a man and carry the heavy shit? Besides, I'm twice your size. How much attention do you think we'll attract if I'm skipping alongside you like a princess while you look like a pack mule?"

She couldn't help but laugh at the imagery. Elle reluctantly conceded to his point. "Thank you." She picked up her weapons case and followed him out the door. As they walked to the parking area, she put on her sunglasses and allowed her thoughts to shift to scanning and cataloging everything in her sightline.

CHAPTER 2

The last time she walked around BIAP was years ago, during what was called OPERATION NEW DAWN. Things had looked different then. Most Iraqis thought that once the Americans took down Saddam Hussein there would be a McDonald's and Starbucks on every corner and they would be walking through the streets seeing movie stars everywhere. That was not the case. After ten plus years of war, betrayal, disillusionment, and finally reluctant acceptance, the country started to find its own identity. Of course, Iranian influence and a thousand-year-old hatred inspired by sectarian divides made moving forward together an almost impossible task. Everyone was out for themselves with their own agenda, and everyone expected someone else to take care of them, bad situation all around.

Then came Daesh. Most everyone knew them as ISIS or the Islamic State, but Elle refused to call them that. She would never give them that validation. Elle knew a lot of people thought western civilization created these monsters and persecuted them because of their religion. But she had been face-to-face with enough of those fanatics to know the truth: they were pure evil, operating without conscience or remorse.

She watched a TV show called *The Following* once. It was a story about a charismatic serial killer who created a cult of like-minded individuals all with insatiable blood lust. That is what Daesh was. They masqueraded as a religious group out to create paradise on earth for their people, but they were all about power and money. They got their kicks out of torture, rape, and murder, and then used religion to justify their atrocities.

They took to the internet and started a terror and recruitment campaign on a scale never seen before. And the media outlets ate up the horror and spat it back in the world's face, doing as they'd wanted. Making them famous, feared, and earning them more sympathizers and recruits.

Elle had no doubt that was why she was here. Sent by the CIA to bring down Daesh. When things went genuinely wrong, she was sent in. She knew that she was the last resort, but if exposed she would be painted as the devil incarnate and left to take the fall alone. Elle knew the risks and accepted them. She and Tex made it to the truck. They put the weapons case and bag in the back, and then hopped in with Tex behind the wheel.

She leaned back against the headrest for a minute. Even with her eyes closed, the smell kept reminding her she was in Iraq: dirt, oil, and body odor. After ten minutes of driving around the airfield, they came to a compound with its own security checkpoint. They waited for the guard to give them the signal to approach and then moved forward. Tex handed two security identification badges to the armed guard and waited while he compared the pictures to their faces. After a moment, the guard signaled to his counterpart, who then opened the gate. The guard returned their badges. Tex thanked him and drove through.

Once on the compound, they pulled up to a small, wooden building that had a porch with a few beat-up lawn chairs, a card table, and an old grill on it—an attempt at looking homey. The front door was cypher protected. Inside the main entrance, Tex put her bag in an empty alcove along the far wall, and she set her weapons case in front of it. There were five rooms in the building, with the largest being their Operations center.

She walked into the Ops center and looked around. There were four desks with three monitors on each, and four large flat screen TVs on the back wall. One screen was running BBC World News, and another was showing an Intelligence, Surveillance, and Reconnaissance feed, likely from a military drone. Sitting at two of the desks were the two newest members of her team, Jack Paulson and Eve James.

Jack was a computer genius, handsome, and great with gadgets and gizmos but not so much people. Eve was the quintessential girl next door: sweet, charming, adorable, and the best analyst on the planet. They had only been on the team for six months, but Elle liked them both instantly. Tex, whose real name was Mike Traviano, rounded out their team as her second-in-command in charge of all the coordination, logistics, and security. As a former Army Ranger, 75th Regiment, he was the only member with a military background. He was from a large Italian family, but, for some reason, their boss thought he was Mexican. So, they started calling him Tex-Mex, which turned into Tex. She'd known Tex for three years, and there was no one she trusted more, which made him the closest thing to family she had.

Eve squealed and threw her arms around Elle's neck, almost knocking them both over.

"Miss me, kid?"

"Are you kidding me?!? It's been three months. Where have you been? Wait, never mind, I know you won't tell us. But, seriously, you could have called."

"I know it's hard to adjust to the way we do business, but that's part of the deal. You'll get used to it. We team up against impossible odds and then go back to our secret identities when we're done." Elle said.

Eve rolled her eyes, "It seems so dramatic when you say it like that."

"Might as well embrace it, besides I know for a fact that Jack has super hero tights on under his pants." Elle gave Jack a look.

"I'm not wearing tights," Jack declared indignantly, turning red. But after a long, knowing stare from her, he amended his statement. "They're boxer briefs. So, what if they're Batman? They're very masculine."

They all laughed.

"I'll never figure out how you do that, Elle." Jack grumbled. "I swear if you have hidden cameras in my underwear drawer I'm suing."

Tex indicated for Elle to take the chair behind the desk, then perched on the corner of the one next to hers. Once everyone was seated, Tex kicked off the initial report.

"We've been tasked to cripple Daesh. In order to do that, we think that we'll need to strike several serious blows to their support network. All the military targeting in the world is focused on Al-Baghdadi and his Generals up north, but you know the Al-Baghdadi moniker will just get passed to the next asshole who wants to be a famous warlord and pick up the so-called cause. What Eve and Jack have put together shows the real power and threat comes from the money men, spiritual advisors, and media people. We eliminate them, and we think the organization will crumble. Eve will give you the wavetops."

Elle wished it was as simple as Tex made it sound, but as he spoke, her hopes of a short stay vanished.

Taking the cue, Eve piped in. "I'll start with the money men. There are three main ones that are responsible for a majority of the group's cash flow, both the support money coming in and the blood money going out. One of these guys is a major international banker, another is a black-market arms dealer, and the third runs a large hawala network. We suspect that the arms dealer is funneling money to them as well as weapons, but strange as it sounds we think most of the support money is coming from the hawala network. Daesh seems to only use the banker for bribes and recruitment money."

"Where are they currently assessed to be?" Elle asked.

"The banker is in Geneva of all places, the back-market guy is in Djibouti, the only one kinda local is the Hawala operator. He's in Al Qaim." Eve replied.

Elle nodded.

"Next, are the spiritual advisors. I really hate these guys. They are the absolute worst. I can't believe the things they say are justified in the eyes of God and required to be good Muslims. Did you hear what they did to that village up north, the Pagan—"

Elle cleared her throat.

"Sorry, Elle. Anyway, there are dozens of these so-called religious scholars advising members of Daesh and coming up with new fatwas against humanity. So, it was really difficult trying to narrow down centers of gravity, but I think I have it down to five. Each of these men are trusted to hold all the religious zealots together and make certain their brand of crazy is directed away from the group's leadership. Two of them are believed to be in Syria right now, but the other three are in Iraq." Eve paused and started shifting her weight from foot to foot.

Elle sighed. She knew Eve hated giving her news that would piss her off and this was her tell. "Just spit it out, Eve."

Tex answered instead. "One of these guys is in Baghdad currently, hiding among the elite in the city. When Eve turned in her preliminary findings, the home office went a little crazy. We've been directed to take him out immediately."

She felt anger settling in, but it was bitter, dangerous. She despised it when the people who paid their bills thought they knew better and decreed a course of action. Every time that had happened, something had gone wrong.

Elle took a deep breath. "Keep going, Eve, we'll come back to this. I want to hear what else you have."

Eve nodded. "The last spoke on this twisted wheel is the media guys. These slimes are the worst of the worst. They monitor websites and put out propaganda as news to entice other like-minded idiots to join their cause or send money. They film the beheadings and package up IED footage like party favors. There are three of these guys who seem to be calling all the shots. For the most part, the Daesh leaders are very cautious around technology even though they exploit the hell out of it, so there aren't many cameras or communications gear around. Everything runs autonomously until they need to make a new proclamation or video. The film guy is currently in Mosul; the two internet leads are here in Baghdad."

She smiled at Eve and Jack. "Thanks. Do I have a copy of your findings?"

Eve pulled some folders from her desk and handed them to her.

"I divided it up into the three groups, but if you want me to break it down differently, I can."

Elle shook her head. "This is fine, Eve, thank you. She flipped through the folders and saw last known photographs, locations, as well as reporting on the targets. Some of the information looked like it was taken directly from personal computers, phone records, and bank accounts. Smiling to herself, Elle relished the advantage her team's talents gave her. It was clear they had learned a lot from their first mission together, hunting some of the CIA's most wanted. People who had been eluding the intelligence community for years. Once found, Elle convinced the targets to become assets.

In two weeks, Eve and Jack had made more progress than the entire U.S. government had in the last few years. But, then, her team didn't care about the laws, regulations, and oversight that kept everyone else fighting with one hand tied behind their backs. War and espionage were traditionally a gentlemen's game. There were unspoken rules and courtesies, and lots of politics that everyone seemed to abide by for the most part. Well, fuck that. Elle and her team weren't gentlemen, and this wasn't conventional warfare. These guys were animals, and, while everyone else was busy being politically correct and trying to negotiate, innocent people were being brutalized and murdered.

"This is perfect, guys. I'll need some time to review and come up with the next move. So, Tex, where am I crashing?"

"I thought about putting you up at the five-star resort up the road but there's a clown convention in town and I didn't think you would want to deal with all the big shoes and animal balloons."

"Very funny. Now, if you don't mind showing me where I can get a shower and some food, I want to spend some time with these files. I intend to have a game plan by tomorrow morning at the latest."

"Underachieving as usual. Fine, slacker, let's go."

CHAPTER 3

She followed Tex to another room decorated with little touches in an attempt to make things look nicer. Elle shook her head, even in a tactical environment, Eve was still trying to be Suzy Homemaker. Wooden braces that functioned as walls divided the room to create two bedrooms.

"You and Eve will be bunking in here. There isn't a shower in this building, but there is a female shower trailer about fifty yards out. I'll show you, and, on the way there, I'll run you by our kitchenette and prep room. It's not much, but it'll do. There is a chow hall that all the SOF guys go to that's a few minutes' walk from here if you don't feel like making yourself anything. I've got a deal with the staff there. We can snag whatever to keep our place stocked so we can minimize our footprint. Of course, they have a pretty impressive gym set up just around the corner, open twenty-four hours. Jack and I are bunking in the room cater-corner to this one."

She took it all in as she followed Tex around the small building. It wasn't much, but it was perfect for their needs. As they went back outside, the sun was starting to go down, and activity in the compound was picking up. Typical, since most operations happened at night. The SOF guys tended to sleep during the day, mainly due to the scorching heat. The rise in activity made her want to finish the tour as quickly as possible to avoid drawing too much attention.

In the predominately male world she frequented, a new female presence would spread like wildfire. The more attractive the woman, the more interest there would be. She could only imagine the stir that Eve had already caused, and her arrival was likely going to double that. Tex walked her around the compound, pointing out each of the various structures and their function. She paid close attention to the areas that would have the most activity and mentally mapped ways to avoid them. Then they were back at their base of operations.

Walking into the ready room again, she went to the alcove that held her gear and pulled out her low-profile body armor and tactical vest and put them on pegs against the wall. Then she grabbed the rest of her bag and weapons case and followed Tex to their prep room, which held their temporary armory. Another cypher lock was on the outside of this door, but this metal door was solid and set into steel reinforced concrete. She paused at that and wondered who had occupied this space before her team had acquired it.

"It belonged to a military intelligence unit during OPERATION IRAQI FREEDOM. I'm sure they used it to store sensitive equipment and not weapons, but it works perfectly for either. The building sat vacant for a while after the major troop withdrawal when the shift to NEW DAWN occurred, but for a little while now the SOF guys have been using it for a recreation area. They had a bunch of TVs and couches and even a damn pool table in here. I think they were a little butt hurt that they lost their *Call of Duty* game room, but they couldn't really argue that it was mission essential."

She smirked. It never got old—Tex answering a question she hadn't yet asked out loud. One thing about the special operations community that never changed was the work hard, play hard, mentality. These guys were the tip of the spear, but that also meant they needed outlets to come down after missions. Sex, alcohol, general destructive behavior, and video games seemed to be the usual. That was why it was critical to keep these guys working and focused. They had a high prey drive that could turn nasty if not given proper outlets.

She walked in and put her weapons case on the table in the center of the room and looked at the walls. One wall had a counter and shelves that had been set up as a fully stocked cleaning station. The second had a selection of rifles, pistols, and grenade launchers all neatly racked and segregated by type.

The third wall had another work bench and various tools, wires, and other components in containers on shelves. She saw boxes that held pinhole cameras and others that held circuit boards and timers. Under the workbench was a small safe; she had no doubt there were several blocks of plastic explosives inside, just in case.

"We're set with all the usual. Ready for bear if need be, but we've got the bells and whistles over here to fabricate whatever devices you request for your subtler approach." Tex stated, gesturing around him.

"Good work, Tex, I appreciate you getting everything set up. Any issues?"

He shook his head. "Nah, we got everything in with one small CONEX box that was buried in a gear shipment for the compound. We got a couple of inquisitive looks while we offloaded, but since everything was in unmarked pelican cases, there wasn't a whole lot of detail for anyone to grasp ahold of. Had a couple of guys offer to help, but we politely declined. Sent Eve out for a jog around the compound and that pretty much ended any interest in us. Jack and I got everything in and got rid of the CONEX before she got back, so by the time she hit the shower everyone had forgotten about us."

"If anyone lays a finger on Eve, they may lose the hand or disappear altogether."

"She was fine."

Elle wasn't appeased.

Tex held up both hands in defeat. "Okay, Mama."

Elle walked to the center table, opened her weapons case, and pulled out her favorite guns: an M4 carbine and MP-5 assault rifle with several suppressors, a Sigsauer P-226, and P-290. Each one had modifications on the grips and sights adjusted to her specifications. Since lives tended to depend on her ability to effectively use her weapons, she was territorial about them. Tex had left a select area of the second wall bare for her, knowing she'd want all her weapons together and separate from the others. She placed them in their new home, then stowed the empty case in the corner. She glanced at the lower shelf and saw multiple ammunition cans, sealed and neatly stacked.

Satisfied, she grabbed her bag and walked back toward her room.

As they passed the entrance to the Ops center, Tex said, "I'm going to hit the chow hall if you guys want to come. They're doing steak and lobster tonight and I don't feel like cooking."

"I'm starving, so, yes," Eve said.

"Lobster in Iraq, doesn't that bother anyone?" Jack asked.

"Shut up, Jack, and get moving. You know you're going to come with us because otherwise you're making yourself something in the kitchen and we all know how that will turn out," Tex turned to Elle and asked, "You want us to wait for you or bring you something back, Mama?"

"If you could snag me something, I would appreciate it. I'm going to unpack and then shower and get started on those files."

"You got it."

She turned into her room and dropped her bag on the floor. She had about a week's worth of daily wear clothes, workout gear, and undergarments in her bag, as well as a few clothes that would help her blend in this type of environment. She got everything as situated as she could in the small space and hung up the special clothes to help the wrinkles fall out. Then she pulled out her iPod and toiletries. She also had an international cell phone that was better encrypted than anything on the market. But that was it. She didn't travel with anything personal other than the iPod. No pictures or little mementos of home or loved ones.

Elle didn't really have a home, not in the way most people did. She had a residence, a couple actually, where she stayed when she wasn't working. Each place was furnished and tastefully decorated and had things in it that belonged to her, but there was nothing of real significance in them. They blended in with her assumed lives at each location. To her neighbors, she gave off the image of a woman that came from money.

She had a residence in the country and one in the city. When she wasn't at one, her neighbors assumed she was at the other, or traveling. It helped to keep up her cover as a photographer. And she did travel the world selling her photographs to publications such as *National Geographic* and *Newsweek*; that just wasn't the whole truth about what she did. Her weapons case looked like it was probably carrying a tripod and camera equipment. Her life itself was an endless shadow game; she was always working from behind the scenes or creating an illusion to distract onlookers while she went about her business.

Elle sat on her bed for a few moments longer, just letting the day's events sink in. Then she gathered her toiletries, towel, shower shoes, and a change of clothes. She put them in a small gym bag and headed out to the shower trailer. As soon as she stepped outside, the hair on the back of her neck stood on end. She was being watched. Since the sun hadn't quite gone down yet, there was still plenty of light to take in the details of her surroundings. She casually glanced around as if nothing was out of the ordinary and caught sight of a group of four men standing outside of the gym door; definitely operators. *Shit.*

They had probably been hoping to catch a glance of Eve, but instead she had walked out and now she was on their radar. It was bound to happen, but it was something she had hoped to avoid for as long as possible. Most of the people she had seen earlier when Tex had taken her around the compound had been techs, support personnel assigned to the SOF mission— less of a problem than the operators since most of them were fairly normal people who tended to give others their space; there were a few type-A personalities in there, but mainly because they were specialists in their field.

Operators, on the other hand, functioned on a different level. They all tended to be type-A, and assertively so. They viewed things a little differently, women in particular. Their gaze was heavy, but she knew she could talk her way out of almost anything. And for those few things she couldn't, she could be deadly. Not wanting to resort to that, she walked nonchalantly to the showers.

CHAPTER 4

Still steaming from the hot water in the shower, Elle got dressed. She looked at herself in the mirror as she used a bottle of water to brush her teeth. She looked tired, and she suddenly felt that way. Jet lag. Elle still hoped to get some time in with the mission files before she succumbed to sleep...caffeine might be necessary. She packed up her stuff and headed out of the trailer. More people were moving around, going to the chow hall she assumed, but she didn't see the same men from earlier. She walked back to their building as quickly as she could without drawing attention to herself.

Once back inside, she felt relieved. She stood for a moment and listened. Her team wasn't back yet, so all she could hear was the news playing in the background. She walked through the Ops center on the way to her bedroom and grabbed the three file folders. Once back in her room she put her stuff away, grabbed a legal pad and pencil, and laid on the bed with the files. Her instincts told her to start with the money men, but since she was being ordered to take out the religious advisor first, she started there. She contemplated ignoring orders and taking care of things her own way, but that would mean increased interference from higher. She knew that her boss was likely receiving pressure from the Pentagon and White House. She would need to figure out a way to take care of the problem with the handicap of not being able to start where she wanted.

She heard the door open and her team's voices coming back in. She walked into the Ops center to her desk, where Tex had set a Styrofoam container. She opened it up and found a small feast of steak, lobster, green beans, and chocolate cake. "Thanks for snagging this. I really appreciate it. Looks good enough that it may not send me running for the shitters later."

Tex laughed. "Yeah, it's not what you would call gourmet, but these guys usually eat pretty good, so its decent. They are growing boys after all. Can't expect to kill things on an empty stomach."

She ate quietly while she enjoyed the banter of her team. Back in her room, she returned to her bed and sat cross-legged and grabbed the file on the religious advisors. Ironic that Eve had uncovered five of them, one for each of the pillars of Islam. She wondered if that had been intentional. She scanned through the pages and numbered each of the targets as she went:

1. Khalid Omar (Imam/Baghdad)
2. Muhammad Walid (Imam/Syria)
3. Mahmud Hussein (Cleric/Syria)
4. Muhammad Kalash (Cleric/Mosul)
5. Uday Satar (Cleric/unknown)

She focused for a few minutes on Number 1, Khalid Omar, since he was the target she had been directed to take out immediately. He was everything she despised and more, which took some of the irritation out of being told how to do her job. She could see why she was being pressured to remove this guy as soon as possible. He was the face of the "cause." He was conservatively responsible for bringing in at least half of their recruits.

Number 1 was charismatic; and cruel. Anyone who he deemed as being unfit was brutalized and killed. Once he got the young recruits into the fold, he required complete submission from them. If they refused, they were punished severely. They either came to heel, or he had them murdered. He was also responsible for presiding over the prayers before each major attack, and he blessed the suicide bombers before they went to martyr themselves.

Khalid was a symbol to them, and the world. That would end soon.

Elle continued reading, still formulating her plan, knowing that she would be expected to take out each group in turn. It was simpler, and more efficient. But in her opinion not nearly as effective. She didn't get called in for half measures, or the easy way. Cold determination was setting in, and she became wholly focused on her new problem. Slowly putting the pieces together; she was going to solve this one way or the other.

The next group was the money men. She definitely would have started with them if she had been free to do so. Continuing with her list, she added:

6. Hans Waite (Banker/ Geneva)

7. Gerard Fior (Black Market/Djibouti)

8. Sallah Huway (Hwallah/Al-Qaim)

Without funding, things would get more complicated for Daesh, which is why you should follow the money first. Unfortunately, since they took over some oil refineries and had corrupt people the world over willing to buy from them, they wouldn't be crippled that way alone. But it was a start.

Reading over the file, she was struck by the seemingly normal profile Hans Waite portrayed. Ol' Number 6 seemed to be your average professional, family man, no indications of what would make him assist a group like this. Something wasn't right there; she was sure of it. She knew Eve's research was spot on, and it conclusively showed that his name and the various accounts he managed were directly tied to Daesh activities, but that was it. No unusual banking activity under his personal or family accounts, no lavish vacations, no known vices or disciplinary issues, not even a parking ticket. It didn't add up. To her, that meant one of two things. Either it was a setup and Waite was a patsy, or he was much more involved and dangerous than they knew. She would need to proceed with caution where Number 6 was concerned. Until she had all the details, she may need to surveil him to get the answers she needed.

Another problem was Gerard Fior, Number 7, ex-French Foreign Legion turned mercenary and black-market arms dealer. Elle wished she could say he was the first one of his kind she'd crossed paths with over the years. He was the perfect example of what she always worried about with the special operations community. They were a different breed. You take away their outlets, and they become destructive. This guy decided to put his skills to use for the highest bidder, and when that didn't do it for him, he took the adrenaline rush and money to the next level. Nothing gets the blood pumping like selling death and destruction to psychopaths willing to kill anything and anyone who gets in their way. Always high risk, high reward, and lots of opportunities for violence.

Merc paradise.

From everything she was seeing, 7 had been one hell of a soldier, but it hadn't been enough for him. He was a man that lived for the thrill, and she could understand that; she did the same. This made him a real threat. She would need to take her time with this one; 7 may need to be a mission all on his own.

On the other hand, Number 8 was exactly the type of target she preferred; lower profile and major impact towards meeting her end goal. The hawala banking system went back to the Templar Knights and was nearly impossible to trace using modern technology. Essentially a person went to a hawala, gave money to be used by someone elsewhere, and that person went to a hawala on the other end and picked it up. It was like Western Union, but without the assistance of technology. It was simple, brilliant, and made tracking sources of funding damn near impossible.

Sallah Huway's location, in a town right on the Syrian border, was not a lucky coincidence either. It was an easily exploited border area between the two countries and a lucrative place to set up shop for anyone who wanted to receive funds for a group who laid claim to both countries. She could probably take him out fairly quickly with a little support from the SOF guys, but she would need to weigh the benefits of that course of action with the aftereffects of being on the radar of the men who went on that mission with her. It'd be a small footprint, but still, at least four more guys would be needed. Depending on the individuals, that could be problem enough.

Finally, she read up on the media men:

9. Victor Morrow (Film/Mosul)

A Brit embedded with these animals, making their movies. He knew there was a wide market for his films, and he enjoyed capturing the suffering prior to death. Before he found his calling working for Daesh, he got arrested for suspicion of circulating snuff films. They could never prove that it was him, so the charges were dropped. He was currently in the group's stronghold in Mosul, and likely having the time of his life plying his trade.

The final two targets held her attention for a while as more of her plan began to take form.

10. Rami Hasar (Cyber/Baghdad)

11. Mufti Assan (Cyber/Baghdad)

They were the masterminds behind the Daesh online campaign. They ran the recruitment sites and posted the propaganda that helped continue to brainwash those too naive to see how easily they were being manipulated, and add fuel for those just looking for a place to unleash their savagery and have it heralded as godly. They worked in tandem it seemed, and had selected Baghdad as their current base of operations.

The location was likely picked since it would be significantly harder to find them amongst the population, and because connectivity to the internet is a little hard to come by when you're being bombed. They were clever, these two. They used internet cafés, piggybacking off unsecured Wi-Fi to do their dirty work. They never seemed to pop up in the same place twice, physically that is. Elle knew there was no way this was their only online presence; they had the cyber world at their fingertips. Guys like this would never stay off the web unless it was because they were off doing other business. The details of her plan were solidifying, but she would need Jack to work some magic.

She looked at her watch; it was close to midnight. Elle put the files and her notes aside and went back out into the Ops center. The lights were mostly out, but she could hear a movie playing. Jack and Eve had pulled their chairs into the center of the room and were sitting in their pajamas, eating popcorn, and watching *Jurassic World*. Tex was still at his desk reading, but his eyes were getting heavy. When he saw her standing in the doorway, he sat up a bit.

"What's up, Mama?"

Jack paused the movie and they all turned.

"Jack, I know its late, but if you're up for it I'd like you to start on something for me tonight. And, Eve, I need something from you, too."

"Of course, Elle."

"I appreciate it. Jack, the two internet leads, Rami and Mufti. I'm going out on a limb that they have a cyber presence outside of their official duties."

Jack perked up. "I can pretty much guarantee it. Most of us have a couple of different profiles out there just to keep things interesting."

"Find them, I want as much of their digital footprint as possible. Try to get me a pattern of life and any associated locations. Eve, I need you to look into our first target some more. I want his routine and who protects him. He likes an audience, and I intend to use that against him. Tex, I bet you haven't slept much since you got here, so get your happy ass to bed. When you get up, I need you to call home and get us access to the Agency's new bird. And we're going to need a flight crew and two shooters."

Tex shook his head, "That's a lot of exposure, Elle, you sure? I can fill one of the shooter spots to limit it more."

"I'll need you running cover and support, you know that. If shit goes sideways, you're all I have, and all that Eve and Jack have to get them out of dodge. You know these guys, and how best to deal with them."

He nodded and got up. "I'll get started on getting you access to the bird first thing tomorrow and then I'll get you a crew. Got a timeline?"

"Tell them Thursday night, but it may shift left or right depending on how the week progresses." It was Monday evening, so that gave her almost three days to get number 1, 10, and 11 taken care of before she set off after Number 8. Short timeline, but she was confident she could make it. "After the op on Thursday, I'm going to want us packed and out of here. By the time word gets around about the mission, we should be gone, and they can be left to wonder."

"Done. Where we heading to next?"

"Djibouti."

Tex looked pained. "Shit, man, why can't we ever find ourselves in Tahiti or something. Do you have any idea how badly that place smells?"

"Sorry, Tex, but the mai tais and bikinis will have to wait until we're done. Then you can go wherever you want to decompress." She turned to Jack and Eve, who were both already working away on their computers. "Do what you can tonight, guys, but I'm going to need you sharp. This problem may take a little longer than anticipated to fix. So, when you need it, sleep. Dump everything you find in a folder for me and I'll go through it on my own."

"We're on it, Elle." Eve said.

"This is going to be fun," Jack said grinning, not even taking his eyes off his screen.

"Don't let them know you're hunting for them, Jack," Elle cautioned.

He turned. "This isn't my first time, Elle. I'm not a child and I don't need a babysitter."

"This from the man wearing *Suicide Squad* pajama bottoms. DC comics should really pay you royalties."

With that, she returned to her room and laid down on the bed. Jet lag was always an issue and she needed to get ahead of it.

CHAPTER 5

She woke a few hours later when Eve finally poured herself into bed. Elle thought about checking up on her; but fought the urge knowing Eve needed to sleep. She lay awake for a little while wondering if she should go ahead and get up and get back to work, but she ended up drifting off again. Elle woke up the second time knowing it was still early morning, even though the sun had not risen yet. She couldn't have gotten more than five hours of sleep, but that was enough for now.

She changed into workout gear and went out to the Ops center. To her surprise, both Jack and Tex were up and working. "What the hell? Did you guys sleep at all?" She noticed the pile of Rip-it cans next to Jack and already knew his answer.

"I did for a little while, but I'm pretty sure the mad professor has been at it all night again." Tex replied.

"Jack, you do know sleep is required for humans or have you given up on keeping up the pretense?" Elle asked.

"I'm hot on their trail, Elle, don't want to lose it now. I'll have everything on these two any minute." He was amped, big time, and caffeine was coursing through his veins, but she could see that he was fully locked on. She left him to it.

Tex pushed back in his chair and looked at her. "Heading to the gym or for a jog?"

"Gym. Figured it should be quiet enough right now to suit me."

"I heard back from home. They're greasing the wheels for us to use the new bird, but they weren't happy about it. Said it seemed like too much."

"I really don't care what they think. Maybe next time they won't interfere if my methods make them unhappy."

He shrugged. "Fuck it. It's not like they have anything better to do with it right now."

She knew the Pentagon was very territorial about their stealth helicopter program, but after part of one of the prototypes ended up blown to shit in Bin Laden's backyard, the cat was kind of out of the bag. Besides, this was what the damn thing was designed for.

"I'm going to need evening prayer time for Thursday, and have Eve find me Sallah Huway's mosque when she gets up. Also, I want an assessment of Khalid Omar—Number 1's intentions tonight and tomorrow. And I'll need a vehicle."

"Will do. I should have a couple of bodies lined up for Thursday by tonight, as well. I assume the usual constraints apply? Snipers with the ability to keep their mouths shut?"

"Tall order, I know, since they're typically so humble, but do what you can," she said.

She left Tex to it and went to the nearby gym. As she walked outside, she was pleased that it appeared to be quiet. Not a whole lot of people out, which hopefully meant there would only be a few people in the gym. Elle walked into the massive structure and looked around. It had likely been a hangar before the war, but now it was a well-stocked and organized gym—lots of treadmills, ellipticals, and about every kind of machine and free weight imaginable. She walked through the main room into a second room with cross fit equipment, punching bags, form dummies, and a large matted area for sparring.

As she took in the gym's furnishings, the back door opened and a man walked in. Her heart stuttered. He was very handsome, classic good looks with broad shoulders and an athletic build. He carried himself like a man who could handle any situation and his expression said he was all business. It wasn't until he looked at her that she realized she had been staring, she couldn't remember how long. Baffled by her strange reaction, she tried to regain her composure. She inclined her head to the man, a polite acknowledgment, and returned to the other room.

It wasn't until she got to an elliptical, she realized she hadn't gleaned anything from him. She had just reacted, and that was it. He was a mystery, and it made her reaction even more unsettling. Who the fuck was that guy and what was wrong with her? Elle felt disconcerted and uncertain, both rare emotions for her. *This is ridiculous. What the hell am I doing?* She knew she couldn't lose sight of what she needed to do, but couldn't stop her thoughts from moving back to the man. She'd never experienced that before and, quite frankly, thought it wasn't possible.

Knowing she needed to clear her head, she left the gym to run around the compound for a while—distance would put things into perspective. As she ran, she started to go over the details that she had read in Eve's report, and thought through her current plan, examining it from multiple angles to make certain this was her best course of action. Her time in Baghdad wouldn't likely have the impact she would have preferred, but since she was working within someone else's constraints, she would have to make the best of it.

By lap three, all extraneous thoughts vanished and she was focused. Elle hoped by the time she showered, ate, and returned to the Ops center; she would have the information from her team she needed. She wanted to be out in the city tonight, but she still needed to hear where two of her targets were going to be.

Returning to their building, she heard Jack yell for her.

She walked into the Ops center. "What've you got?"

"I've found both of them. You were right, Elle, they couldn't resist being online. They have several online personas, but I've managed to trace them back to what I have to assume are their bed down locations. I've pulled up imagery of the locations, and they are apartments in the Karada area south of the Green Zone."

"How do you know it's them?"

"The coding they use is like a fingerprint, and they have a habit of using the same bookmarks when they're writing."

"Good work, Jack. I'll need the locations of their residences. What can you tell me about their day-to-day lives?"

"It doesn't seem like they have much of any life outside of the cyber realm. They seem to be almost constantly online, but less active around the late morning. My guess is that they're up all night and sleep through the day. Most of their posts for the jihadist sites are in the middle of the night and during the early morning hours. Probably to avoid as many eyes as they can while they're out stealing Wi-Fi, and to make sure their content is up before morning prayers."

"Good to know. Give me everything you can find on these guys and then go get some sleep. Tonight, I need you to monitor their activity. When you notice a lull, I want you to hijack their site and continue as if you were them. Can you do that?"

Jack seemed affronted. "Of course, I can do that. But they'll know something is wrong almost immediately, Elle. Even someone who is a little computer savvy would be able to cut my access and then use the incident to fuel more bullshit propaganda. I suppose at that time they may be too drowsy to realize anything right away but...." He trailed off. When he saw the look on her face, comprehension seemed to hit, and "oh" was all he managed.

"I intend to make certain they don't notice anything, ever again," she said bluntly.

"As you monitor the way they do business, make sure you can get into and out of all their Daesh affiliated websites and that you can mimic their fist and script perfectly. Also, get your voice editing software ready. By tomorrow night, I'll have some video footage for you to adjust the audio on. In the meantime, get some sleep. You'll be working tonight."

Jack started to protest but nodded instead. He finished compiling his notes then walked to the room he shared with Tex. Elle went to her room to get her things for the shower and a change of clothes. Eve was still asleep, so she made sure to be quiet. As she walked to the shower trailer, she noticed more people walking around—probably the night crew grabbing food before heading off to sleep. Elle showered and headed back. She stopped in the kitchenette and grabbed some Pop-Tarts, and then went to her desk to review what Jack and Eve had left for her.

Target Number 1 was in the Karada District just like Numbers 10 and 11, but for a much different purpose. It seemed that Number 1 was in town on a recruiting drive of sorts. He was meeting with several of the more influential members of the Iraqi business community and politicians. Most of these guys were opportunists in the basest sense of the word. They survived the war and regime changes by being friends with anyone who would pay them. These men had no loyalty to anyone but themselves, but they did everything they could so all sides saw them as valuable. It was the coward's way out, but in this environment, it paid dividends. For now, at least.

These were some of the wealthiest and most connected individuals in the country. There could only be one reason for Number 1 to be there. He was making a sales pitch to gain support for Daesh in central Iraq. The terrorist group may have Northern Iraq in its clutches, but the capital was a different story. Run by Shia Muslims, and with Iranian backing, they were not about to bend to the desires of Sunni Muslims. Daesh was attempting another avenue to expand its influence by using the Sunni elite to tempt the Sunni majority of the city to its cause.

They were meeting at the residence of one of the most prominent businessmen in the country; it was essentially a compound all to itself—a small palace with high walls on each side and a main gate. The owner reportedly kept a small security force on the premise, likely to guard against thieves and other criminals. She studied the schematic that her team had left in the folder as well as the overhead imagery of the area. It would not be easy to gain entry, but she would figure it out.

She also studied known photographs of all the men who would likely be at the residence, including her target. He was a tall man with a full beard and mustache and black eyes. He looked exactly like a holy man should, which was why he was so valuable to the group. Add in some sociopathic tendencies with a fanatic flavor and he was the perfect front man for Daesh. She paid special attention to key details of his facial structure and any personal items he had in the picture; she noticed books were a common theme in her target's photos.

Elle went to the armory's fabrication bench and searched the containers until she found what she was looking for: pinhole cameras. She selected six and began testing them to ensure they were functioning properly and had enough battery life for several days. She needed about twenty-four hours of recording time, but she wanted to make certain that if circumstances changed they would continue to operate until she could retrieve them.

These cameras had a very small main body with the camera itself being at the end of a fiber optic cable. This allowed for flexibility with hiding the components and angling the lens. There were smaller options that would be much easier to conceal, but the memory life wouldn't be what she needed. Elle packed away the cameras in a zippered bag to protect them and then added a small tool kit and several different types of fasteners and tapes to her inventory of items she would need. She would have to hide the cameras as quickly and effectively as possible, and, without knowing what was inside each of the rooms, that was going to be a challenge.

Next, she walked over to her weapons case and opened the side pocket to remove her knife and lock pick set. She also pulled her SIG P-290 from the wall and loaded a magazine. Elle didn't intend to use the weapon tonight, but better to have it and not need it, then to not have it when things went wrong. She stood and contemplated the other items in the room and decided that she was ready; so, she returned to her room to send an encoded message to a couple of assets and get some more sleep. Now that she had a plan and knew where she needed to go, she needed to rest.

It was going to be a long night.

CHAPTER 6

When Elle woke up, she checked her watch, almost 1700. Good, there would be plenty of time to finish her prep. Checking her phone, she saw responses to the coded messages she sent earlier; her assets were standing by for further instructions. As she walked past the Ops center, she saw her whole team was there. She nodded in passing. Tex caught up to her just outside the building.

"Got you a vehicle, hope it will work." He turned his head, and she followed his gaze to a grey Honda Civic that was a few years old.

She chuckled. "Looks like I'll be riding in style."

"You have no idea. Check her out."

She walked over and noticed that the tires seemed just a little different for some reason and the windows looked a little thicker. At first, she thought it might be a trick of the light. "It's bulletproof, isn't it?"

"Yep. Had to pull a few strings to get her, but I figured just in case you run into anything unexpected. She'll disappear into traffic around here, too, and no one will give her a second glance."

Elle walked around the car and took in the size of the trunk. Opening it up, she sighed. Well, she would make due. Hopefully, her passengers wouldn't be too big. "Thanks for getting this. Any luck with the rest?"

"Yeah, the Commander of the unit here ponied up two bodies for you. He wasn't happy about it since I wouldn't tell him anything, but the orders pushed through the Pentagon to support with 'no questions asked' won. He said he would give us his two best, and that we better bring them back in one piece."

She inclined her head to him. "Good, I'll want them ready to go at 1800 on Thursday. I'll have you brief them for the op at that point and then I want the bird to be ready for an 1830 departure. I'll join the group right before we take off to minimize their chance to ask questions."

"You going to tell me what the plan is?"

"Yes, but right now I need to piss and get something to eat. We'll chat later."

He laughed. "Don't let me keep you then, and Eve has food waiting for you in the kitchen, so you don't have to hit the chow hall."

She smiled. "Good to know. Be back in a few."

Returning, she went directly to their little kitchen and saw the box in the refrigerator that Eve had written her name on.

"It's steak and green beans," Eve said from behind her. "And there is another one with some fruit in it."

"Thanks, I really appreciate it."

"No problem. We'll be in the other room whenever you are ready. I have the maps up on the screen for you, and Jack has the latest on checkpoint locations."

"You read my mind," she said.

"Well, we do pay attention." Eve turned to go, but then paused and added, "There is a box with dessert too if you want it."

"I think I'll hold on to that until I get back. Make sure the boys don't touch it...or else."

Eve laughed.

On the center screen, her team had the three locations she needed marked on the map and had highlighted several routes that would help her avoid checkpoints. As she studied the map and listened to what they told her about security postures, her plan finalized.

"Great work, guys; as always. I'll be heading out shortly to take advantage of evening prayer time, and I intend to be out all night. Jack, I need you on your A game tonight. Once you see that 10 and 11 are showing a lull in activity, I need you to take over the sites and masquerade as them. You need to use their identities to plant subversive ideas into their network. I need both you and Eve to pull from any conspiracy theories about Daesh coming from other Islamic groups as inspiration and draft posts that suggest 10 and 11 may be able to prove the theories are true. It needs to be subtle for now, but with just enough substance to make those reading it uncomfortable. Can you do that?"

Eve and Jack exchanged a short glance. Elle knew this was new territory for them, being actively engaged like this was not something she had asked before.

"Hell, I'll be better at being them then they are," Jack said.

Eve snorted. "You'll definitely need my help. You can't even spell subtle. We can do this, Elle, we won't let you down."

"Tex, I need you to finish prep for Thursday and then start making arrangements for us to be out of here Friday night and on the way to Djibouti."

"Seriously? That's my task? How about something a little more interesting for a change?"

She regarded him for a long time. She always worked alone, but she could use him on this mission. Elle cared what happened to Tex, but he could handle himself, better than most, and she had complete confidence in his abilities.

"I would use you, but then no one would be here to shield Jack and Eve and finish prepping. Besides, I've already activated assets to back me when I need them."

"Elle, they're in the middle of a heavily guarded compound behind a locked door. I think Jack and Eve can keep their heads down for one night. As for the coordination, Thursday is almost complete, and I'll get the Djibouti part taken care of now. If you could use me, then damn it, take me. I'm a part of this team, too, I know what I signed up for."

It seemed like no one in the room was breathing waiting for her to respond. Her team knew this was a major departure for her. Her target wasn't as clear cut as usual, and the interference from their leadership complicated things more. If she didn't evolve, she might become a casualty of her own stubbornness.

"Fine, I want you to be ready to go in thirty minutes. Dress like an Iraqi businessman after hours. Slacks, button-down shirt, loafers. Slick your hair back and wear your ankle holster. We'll need to grab a couple of shovels and tarps for the trunk."

Tex was up on his feet and out the door in seconds. Jack started typing away and Eve put on some coffee and started pulling up her research to expand on the threads from the Islamic opposition that painted Daesh as corrupt.

Elle returned to her room and sat on her bed for a moment and listened to her heart pound. *Is this a mistake?* Was she pulling her team further into the line of fire with her? Was she making a mistake by changing things at the last minute? Should she tell them she changed her mind and go back to her original plan? Elle felt selfish and cowardly suddenly.

She got up and started getting ready for her mission. It was going to be a long one, but there was solace in the routine of getting ready. Elle chose everything very carefully for her work, including her clothing. She pulled out her favorite mission gear. A black, long-sleeved shirt and pants made from a light, flexible, but sturdy cotton blend material that fit her like a second skin. There were zippered pockets on the arms, thighs, and calves for storage. The material was not restrictive in any way but moved with her body and left no material hanging freely to get caught in tight spaces. Several of the seams had been replaced with very thin titanium wire, just in case she ended up stripped of her weapons and tools.

She retrieved her knife from under her pillow and hooked it into her pants at the small of her back. The knife was all black, with a tactical grip, a wicked looking serrated blade that was scalpel sharp with blood grooves, and a glass breaker tip on the end of the handle. It had proven valuable on more occasions than she could count. She went everywhere with it. Next, she put on an ankle holster for her SIG, then went to retrieve the burka hanging on the wall. She pulled the garment on and pulled her hair into a tight bun to ensure that it did not stray out from under the headscarf. Her face would be fully covered except for her eyes. Since they were gray, the lighting of the evening would make it very difficult for anyone to get their shade correct. For now, she let the scarf lay around her shoulders.

She left her room and moved to the armory. Tex was already there. She grabbed her SIG P-290 and the bag with her cameras and tools in it. She secured the small bag under the burka and positioned it so that it would not make an odd bulge.

"All set when you are, Mama."

She looked at her watch and looked at him; he mirrored her, knowing what she wanted. She gave him a second to get his watch ready, and then said, "I have 1830 in five, four, three, two, one, mark." Watches synchronized, she looked him over. He looked the part except that he had a significantly larger build than most Iraqis. His skin tone, coupled with his dress and the waning light, would help him blend in effectively, though. Together, no one would pay much attention to them.

"How's your Arabic these days? Been a while since you've really had to use it."

"Been getting back into the rhythm since we've been here. With all the Arabs running around this base, I've been able to scrape off some of the rust. Not going to be negotiating world peace or trade agreements any time soon, but it's passable for your average guy on the street."

"Good, hopefully we won't need it, but I can't exactly jump in and speak before you do. That would highlight both of us." With most Muslims in Iraq, she would be expected to remain silent unless specifically addressed, and, even at that, sometimes only with a male relative's permission. Most men would avoid pressing her about anything. Add in Tex's size, and she would likely disappear from anyone's interest.

"So, what's the plan?"

"When we leave here we're going to take the southern route around the city and come up to the Karada District from the south east. We'll hit a choke point when we cross the Tigris, but the focus for security is north now, so south is where they are weakest. It'll lengthen the drive, but we need the anonymity both into the district and definitely on the way out. First stop will be the house where Number 1 is staying."

"Wow, you don't waste any time. We taking him out tonight?" Tex seemed surprised.

"Not yet, I'm just paying the house a visit. I want to get some cameras set while everyone is either at prayer, or while the guards are less alert because there will be a fewer people on the streets at that time. I'm betting that they'll be a little bored and complacent."

"What if they aren't, Elle? That's a lot of assumptions."

"Everything I've read about these guys says they're all about the show and not about substance. They would hire a force to look intimidating, but it's a status thing, not so much an actual threat. They're comfortable in their position and believe that their status alone shields them. It's all just business to them."

Tex listened carefully. He wasn't comfortable with it. "What if you get someone who isn't just playing security?"

"I always plan for that possibility. That's why I'm still alive."

He nodded.

"There's a market three blocks away from the house. You'll park there. Then we'll walk until we pass the residence, where I'll break away and you'll find yourself a spot with line of sight to the compound." She opened one of the containers at the workbench and pulled out the small radios and earbuds and handed one to Tex.

"You will be my eyes on major movement or lack thereof. I'm betting that with the Imam in the residence, there will be an unusual adherence to prayer on the property. But I don't think Number 1 is ready to expose himself out in public right now. He knows he's a wanted man. Being so close to a base that has U.S. military on it, he'll hold prayer inside the residence to limit the chances of them positively identifying his location. That will give me a window of time to plant cameras in the office and the bedrooms."

Tex started. "You're going to break in while everyone is there? That's the plan?" he asked.

"It's no crazier than usual. You wanted to play, so you are either in or out."

He cursed under his breath. "You know I'm in."

"Conventional gets you nowhere," she said.

"Fine, I'll be your lookout. Then what?"

"You're also my only backup if shit goes sideways, so stay frosty. But if everything goes smoothly, when I come out we will walk back to the car together and move on to the next location, the apartment of Number 10."

"You make it sound so simple."

"It should be, as long as no one gets too nosey."

Tex snorted.

"10 is an online gambler, he can't be away from his personal computer too long. He seems to go through a pattern of gambling for a couple of hours and then goes to another location to pirate Wi-Fi and do his work with Daesh. He will be much easier to locate and eliminate. Once we arrive in his neighborhood, we will park the car near the apartments and I will check to see if he's inside. If he's not, we wait. Depending on the occupancy of the building, I will either take him out when he returns, or we will follow him to his next location and do it there. It will need to be quick, clean, and silent. His body will go into the trunk until we can dispose of it on the way out of the district."

"What are we going to do with him?" Tex asked.

"He's going to find his eternity in one of the trash fields that scatter this place. We'll select the best option on the route in." She shifted her position to lean on the workbench. "Then comes Number 11. He's a little trickier. Seems he really enjoys his job and spends the evening out all over the city. He's a traveler that one. We may have to wait for him to come home right before the sun comes up, which puts us at the most risk, both for taking him out and burying him."

"Can't we just dump him in the Tigris?"

"Too much of a chance that he'll float. Even if we weigh down the body, the water levels change too much there. For this to work, I need him to disappear."

"Okay, so let's do this," he said.

"One last thing, Tex. I know this goes against every instinct you have, but I need you to do exactly what I say when I say it. Don't get any crazy ideas about being chivalrous or macho while we're out there because it could get one or both of us killed. I normally operate alone for that reason."

He nodded. "This is your show, but I know I can help you, Elle. I won't be a problem."

She felt a sense of awe that he would make that concession. "Alright, let's get moving."

CHAPTER 7

They walked back into the Ops center to check on Jack and Eve. "Keep a low profile, guys. Jack, you ready for this?"

"A walk in the park."

"Don't get cocky, Jack, I need you to keep running their sites. I need it to look like they're still operating as normal, that means masking your location as well."

"I'm all over this, Elle. I'm working through so many different systems they'll never find me, and I'd know I was being traced before they could narrow the field. This isn't my first rodeo."

"Fine. Watch 10 closely since he's going to disappear from the net first, then 11. Eve, please feed Jack what he needs to build a foundation of doubt in the Daesh followers. We're going to be working on this for a while so build slowly. We'll help give it a big push soon enough."

"Of course, Elle. But please be careful out there. You, too, Tex." Eve looked anxious and fidgety.

She embraced Eve and then ruffled Jack's hair and said, "Alright kids, be good."

Tex hugged Eve and punched Jack in the shoulder and then followed her out. Elle did a quick survey of the people outside as she moved to the car. They had caught a break in activity, probably the main chow time; lucky them. She got into the passenger seat as Tex slid into the driver's seat. "You good with the route?"

"Yeah, but I've got a GPS in the glovebox, too, just in case."

She didn't want the GPS active during this evening at all, definitely not when they left the base. The system would catalog their movement. Even if they deleted the log it was an electronic footprint she didn't want, but she understood the redundancy. Who knew what the roads would look like in reality, or if they would be passable. They pulled out of the compound and got a few odd looks from the gate guards, but they got over it quickly and allowed them to leave.

Back out on the main base, it was time to put on the headscarf. Elle didn't like the feeling of the material wrapped around her face but it was necessary. If there were any eyes on or outside the installation watching movement, they would not raise too much interest. She was just a local woman traveling with a local man, probably base workers.

As they drove, she took out her iPod and put in her headphones. Tex glanced at her, then went back to watching the road. "Going to be a quiet ride, huh?" he asked.

She paused; she hadn't considered this part of the mission. Her routine was like breathing to her, but now she was sharing it with a member of her team for the first time. What all did that entail? She sighed and tried to work it out verbally so that he didn't feel left out. "I usually listen to music on the way to a mission. It helps focus and put me in the correct frame of mind, and it energizes me. Since I'm typically working alone, I never really gave much thought to what kind of conversations or what else I might do if someone were to travel with me, at least not one who knew what my end goal was."

"What kind of music?"

"Rock, the harder the better. Makes me feel like a badass."

He started laughing. "Yeah, I bet you don't turn around when things explode behind you. That is the true test of a badass."

She smiled wryly. "Well, I knew when the last few were going to go off, does that count?"

"I suppose, but it is kinda cheating. There is an audio cord in the glove compartment, if you don't mind sharing. I can't sing for shit though, be warned. It might mess with your mojo."

She thought about it for a moment. "What the hell."

She plugged in the device and music filled the car. She put it on shuffle and knew this playlist had a heavier mix, exactly what she wanted. Groups like Slipknot and Five Finger Death Punch intermixed with Halestorm, Metallica, AC/DC, and Guns 'N' Roses. She could feel the energy of the music as they drove. She was getting ready for the challenges to come.

As they moved along the highway off the military base, the view changed from one of concrete to desert with splotches of green. Houses dotted the landscape, some had fared better than others during the war and it was obvious. Every so often there would be a trash field and shacks built to house families displaced during the many years of conflict. The sky was just losing the last of the orange tint on the horizon and a deeper blue was settling around them.

They veered south, and things changed again. The houses butted up to the street with their haphazard fences made of whatever their owners could find. They all crowded on top of each other, and so did the market areas. Butchers had bloody meat on old tables in front of their stores, electronics and textile merchants had gaudy signs that, while effective at drawing the eye, failed to inspire her to want to shop. Trash and people selling bottles of water and containers of gasoline were everywhere.

She wondered what it would have been like to see Baghdad before the war. Structures that once were beautiful, were now falling apart and filthy. Living under Saddam had been terrible in many ways for the Iraqi people. And, one of the side effects of having your life dictated for you is an inability to function independently once free from the reign. Things as simple as cleaning up became a major issue. The government always took care of everything. Now, there were no trash services; people just dumped it in the street.

About twenty minutes into their trip, she saw what she had hoped to find. "Look to your right, Tex. See that trash field?"

He glanced over and shook his head. "That where our internet weenies are going?"

"Yep, we're about ten minutes outside of Karada from here, so there's a risk we could get stopped with two bodies in the trunk before we make it back. But that field is perfect for what we need. I see a burn pit going already. We bury them in it, throw piles of trash in on top of them, and let it all keep burning. No one is going to think twice about the smell or go digging around. The trash is piled so high in that field already we'll have all the concealment we need."

Tex took another look, "What do we do with the car?"

"There's always a path people use to drive into these fields, usually something that breaks off from the road. There." She pointed. Off a dirt road, she could see grooves that showed where people had been driving their trash out to the burn pit. "We should still have some cover of darkness to distort what we are doing from any onlookers. We'll need to be fast."

"Well, I suppose that will be my workout for the day, lifting a couple hundred pounds of shit."

Elle went back to surveying her surroundings, trying to catalog every detail. She watched the way the locals were acting, whether anyone seemed interested in them, and the layout of the villages they passed. It seemed that life was trying to come back to the area, even if it wasn't what it was before. Kids were out playing with soccer balls, and men sat in small groups smoking and talking. Ahead of them, traffic seemed to be getting a little heavier. They must be nearing the bridge.

The Tigris was one of two rivers that flowed through Iraq, and this was the biggest risk to them on their route, but it had to be done. As they got closer to the bridge, she could see there seemed to be a security checkpoint ahead. Exactly what she hoped to avoid.

"Damn it, looks like a snap vehicle check point ahead. You ready to act bored?"

Tex laughed. "What do you mean act?"

She reached into the glove box and pulled out their forged Iraqi Gensia's. They were exact replicas of the required identification documents. Not that it would matter too much. Since there is no standard for the paperwork, unless there's a substantial mistake on them it's almost impossible to know which ones are not legitimate.

"Ahmad and Jasirah Hasan," She read out loud. "Both born in Hadithah. You're thirty-four and I'm twenty-seven according to this."

"I make thirty-four look good, but I think they were being kind with giving you twenty-seven. Not sure you can pull that off."

She gave him the finger, then checked the mirror to make certain her scarf was adjusted properly. She would remain silent through this but wanted to make sure there was nothing a security member would see that would raise interest in them. With only her eyes showing, she should be fine. Her skin complexion was probably a little too tanned but with the nighttime shadows, she hoped it wouldn't be noticeable.

As they got to be a few cars away from the checkpoint, she unplugged the iPod and switched the radio to softly play Arabic music. She sat meekly next to her "husband" and made certain not to make eye contact with any of the men at the checkpoint. The one checking the IDs seemed to be taking his job somewhat seriously, but it appeared that the rest of his crew was bored. She didn't detect any edginess in the group, which was perfect. The likelihood that someone would scrutinize them to have something to do was minimal. All they had to do was not raise the ID checker's interest and they were home free.

As they moved forward, Tex started to roll the window down. It got stuck about three-quarters of the way. Tex used it to his advantage and started cursing at the car under his breath in Arabic as he made it to the man. He apologized as he handed the man the paperwork, and kept fussing with the window.

The security man took the paperwork and smirked. "Been a problem long?"

"Since I got it," Tex grumbled.

"Take it to a mechanic, my brother would give you a good price," the man replied.

"No, I can fix it. Not going to waste money on something like this."

The man glanced at their paperwork, then at Elle. She sat quietly with her hands in her lap. He looked back at the IDs and handed them to Tex. "Good luck with that."

"If Allah wills it." Tex pulled away slowly.

She kept her eyes on the rearview window for a few minutes to make certain they were clear. "Good job, Tex."

"Figured if I was going to talk, might as well stick to things I know best, cars and cussing."

She smiled and inclined her head to him. As they crossed the Tigris, she took a moment to marvel at it. In the evening light, the water looked inviting and cool. In the daylight, the trash along the bank would be plainly visible, and the water would be murky and mud colored. For now, it was like seeing Baghdad as it once was.

On the other side of the bridge, it was immediately apparent that they were in a very different part of town. Even without the flattering lighting, the Karada District was cleaner and in much better repair than anything they had seen so far. The storefronts were well tended, and residences were in good condition. As they progressed through the area, the vehicles were newer models, and the people on the street seemed to be better dressed. It was getting close to evening prayer, so there was a lot of activity on the streets. They moved with the flow of traffic and gradually made their way to the western part of the district where Number 1 was staying with his new associates. The residences here were upscale in comparison to everything they had passed and grander with perimeter walls, making small compounds for their owners.

Within a few moments of entering the area, they saw the market, their starting point. It was busy and would provide the perfect cover for them to disappear into the crowd and slip away. Tex navigated through a dirt lot that served as parking for the market and claimed a spot. Before getting out of the vehicle, Elle took a deep breath and rechecked her headscarf. It was show time. She met her own eyes in the mirror and felt her senses heighten. Everything seemed to slow down. She felt her emotions evaporate and focused determination take over.

CHAPTER 8

Elle got out of the car and fell in behind Tex as he made his way through the market. She kept her eyes cast downward, but she used her peripheral vision to maintain situational awareness. Commerce was going on to her left and traffic was flowing slowly on her right. She smelled the body odor of the people crowded together. Most Iraqis did not wear deodorant, just heavy perfume. She heard people barter for better prices for goods and order food, while groups of men discussed politics and business. It was a good time for everyone to be outside. It was still humid, but now that the sun had gone down the temperature had dropped. As the evening progressed it would drop more, but for now it was as pleasant as it would get.

Tex maneuvered his way through the crowd, and she followed closely behind, so far everything was going according to plan. Anyone who glanced their way was more interested in Tex's size than in her, and that was good for now. They had no interest in engaging with the large stranger, but he would also stick out in their memory. She needed to make sure nothing she did tonight would cause anyone to recall them and potentially connect the dots.

Two men were going to die tonight, but if it was done the way she intended, no one would notice their disappearance for quite some time. But that was later; they needed to take care of their first task of the evening.

They broke through the main body of people around the market and kept moving. The night felt different now that they were away from the crowd—colder, more watchful.

Elle and Tex maneuvered into the elite part of town. Lighting was sporadic, but it was in better repair than anywhere else. You could see some lights on inside the residences. But the most important thing to her was the shadows—the dark pools provided her with the freedom of movement she needed.

After a few minutes of walking, they arrived at the target residence. They did not slow their pace and did not act as though they had any interest in the location at all as they walked by. Elle saw two guards by the front door. By the way they were watching the yard, she knew there was at least one roving guard conducting patrols around the property. The inside of the house was ablaze, which bathed the yard within the fence with light. But the height of the perimeter fence created a massive blind spot. The occupants she could see, appeared so confident and comfortable inside, so free of outside threats.

That was to her advantage.

The fence was stone, and in good condition. That was a rarity in the area, and it told Elle how wealthy the occupants were. The smooth stone would be problematic, but not impossible. The Merrell minimalist running shoes she wore would help her feel for the inevitable crevices that she would need to scale the wall.

After passing the property, they waited until they were out of the line of sight to separate. Without speaking, they both did a quick canvass of the area and took advantage of the break in people to move to their next position without notice. There appeared to be a hookah bar ahead, and Tex made for it. It would give him a partial view of the front of the target building, and that was the most she could hope for. He would be able to tell her about any major movements coming from that way. The rest was up to her.

As Elle moved down an alley that bisected the block of houses they were on, she heard Tex's voice in her ear. "Comms check."

Not wanting to chance making any noise, she keyed her radio twice.

Tex responded, "Two clicks heard, good comms check."

Elle slowed her pace to study her surroundings. She needed to make sure she could disappear without anyone being the wiser. The walls in the alley were in various states of repair; but they were mostly intact. Each residence had their version of a perimeter fence, and that created breaks in the walls and natural recesses. She found one that was completely in shadow and moved into it. She heard rustling inside the narrow space and was startled. Her eyes had not completely adjusted to the dark yet, and she froze while trying to identify what had made the noise.

Whatever had made the sound had frozen; as well.

She inhaled deeply and could only smell spoiled food and dirt. That did not help—that could cover almost anything. The noise came again, very tentative and low to the ground. *Animal. But what kind?* The Iraqi Security Forces routinely slaughtered most of the feral dogs in Baghdad, but that didn't mean she hadn't stumbled onto one. That could be very problematic. They were starving, wild, and since Iraqis hated dogs and abused them, they tended to hate people. She didn't want to have to kill an animal, but she would.

Her eyes adjusted, and she focused on the movement. It was a cat. She moved slowly hoping to influence the cat to run away without making a ruckus.

The last thing she needed was to have it tear off and make all kinds of noise. While animals digging through trash was normal, loud noises would still draw unwanted attention. She pulled off the headscarf and burka. Elle folded them into a hole in the wall and placed a black skull cap over her hair. She made sure each move was deliberate and silent. The cat kept rummaging through the trash, likely too hungry to care about her.

She looked at the narrow pathway and could see it was littered with trash. The residents must have decided that if they couldn't see it, that was good enough. It was not going to be a pleasant trip, and she would need to be very careful not to end up covered in something foul. She didn't need a stench drawing attention to her while she was inside the target residence.

Elle moved along the narrow passageway methodically, as best as she could in the darkness. Time was a factor she couldn't control; she needed to make it to the house quickly. Call to prayer was coming and that timeframe was going to be her best shot at getting this done.

The trip through the passageway seemed to take forever, but it was getting brighter ahead, and the wall was higher. The target perimeter was finally in front of her. She reached the corner and saw that the area was a little more exposed than she'd anticipated from the overhead imagery. While the neighboring structures were more high-end than the rest of the Karada District, they did not have the air of opulence or project wealth in the same way her target's structure did. Mostly, the lighting was more subdued, and there was no obvious security. It would be a risk, but she trusted her instincts that there were no immediate threats.

Her attention returned to the fence, she ran her hands over the stone; this side had not received the same amount of attention as the front. The workers who built it cut corners knowing the occupants would never come back here to check. *Good.* The hastily completed wall had numerous toe and finger holds, but the stone was brittle. She would need to be careful. Elle hoped to use the adjacent property wall as a brace to help her scale the target compound, but it was too far away. She didn't have any other option; she would have to muscle herself up.

She found a groove for her foot about three feet up. Elle knew that in a few minutes the call to prayer would sound. People all over Baghdad would make their way to the mosques, and, if her assessments were correct, her target would make a big showing inside the residence. He would have the occupants come together and lead them through their prayers. Of course, the occupants would go along with it regardless of their beliefs. They would not want to give the impression they were not good Muslims in front of a religious zealot.

The security personnel would likely participate in their own way, probably with prayer rugs at their designated watch positions. And for those who were not religious, she was counting on their complacency—being hired for appearances and not effectiveness.

She was almost at the top of the wall when the call to prayer sounded. It was louder than expected. It was a jolt, and her left-hand hold crumpled under her grip. She barely managed to hook her right hand over the top and prevent a fall. Elle remained still for a moment to listen for any alerting noises and regain her equilibrium. It didn't seem as though the sound had been heard over the singing. She took a deep breath and shifted her hands on the top of the wall, bettering her grip. She inched her head up to get a visual, listening for any indication that someone was nearby or had spotted her.

Nothing.

She scanned the compound. There were two guards at the back, and, just as she predicted, one was rolling out his prayer rug on the stone patio, and the other was pacing and taking a cigarette break. She would have her window soon.

As much as she hated the exposure, her primal instincts screamed to move quickly, her training and experience took over. Her muscles strained with effort, but she very slowly pulled herself on top of the wall. Inch, by painstaking inch, she moved until she laid flat against the stone. If no one stared in her direction for too long, and she remained still, she would blend with the shadows. The guard's night vision would be nonexistent since they were standing in the light of the residence.

The compound was expansive, but she saw what she had hoped for—cars. Not the broken-down junk that one typically saw, but well-maintained Mercedes and BMWs. The vehicles of the guests and the property owners parked valet style one after the other, away from the view of any passersby. It gave security personnel a chance to check them for anything that might be a threat or of interest—any detail that would help the resident businessman take full advantage in his dealings.

She was about ten yards away from the nearest car, a challenge but doable. Elle was fortunate that they kept the cars as close to the wall as they did. She watched the man pacing, studied his mannerisms and timed his movements. Once she was certain about her move, Elle glanced over at the man praying; he was on his knees facing east. His peripheral vision would pick up her movement, so she would need to wait until he was in full prayer position and his forehead was down on the mat.

Elle waited until she would be in the blind spot of both men then rolled off the top of the wall. She rotated her body to get her feet under her and kept the momentum of the fall propelling her forward. The second her feet touched the ground, she allowed her knees to buckle and tucked her body into a forward roll. The fall was not pleasant, but she knew how to absorb the impact of the drop and use it to move forward without breaking any bones. She didn't fight the movement knowing that would guarantee injury; she used it.

Giving herself up to gravity was always unsettling, but she learned how to fall over the years. When her momentum faded, she sprawled flat on the ground to get her bearings before moving again. She was in the blind spot created by the cars, and the two guards would not be able to see her, but any roving patrol coming around the side of the residence might. Elle looked around then army-crawled to the back of the closest vehicle and slid under it. Then she re-examined the guards and the house.

There were multiple windows on the ground floor, but it was highly doubtful that any of them would be open. However, the second floor and the roof would be different. Most locals liked to open the windows at night to avoid high electricity bills. These guys wouldn't care about the cost, but it was likely that they opened the windows to enjoy the air flow. The roof would have chairs and tables for them to take advantage of the view and nighttime air. She looked at the architecture of the building and measured her options. There was an architectural feature that looked like a small ledge, reminding her of crown molding. It ran around the second floor. *That could be useful.*

She looked back at the guards, and another option occurred to her—it was crazy but—she would use the back door.

Watching the men, she planned her steps and evaluated each movement. She continued crawling under the cars and moved to the one closest to the house on the west side. Elle was counting on the probability that the door would be open; she trusted her gut. Moving out from under the car and into a low crouch, she listened for any clue that someone could be coming from around the side of the house. She heard the ambient noise of the night and the movement of the two guards that were now on her left. She would need to move quickly and silently across the open ground to avoid exposure at the corner of the building from anyone coming around from the front.

Ready to move, she took one last look and saw the slightest darkening of a shadow near the front of the house. It was her only warning. She melted back to the ground and lay prone beside the car as the roving guard turned the corner. Then inched her way back under the car, fighting the urge to hurry. She was in the open but the shadows were cloaking her. The guard was busy trying to light a cigarette; she needed to keep from catching his attention. The flame would make it nearly impossible for him to make her out for a few seconds, and she used that window of opportunity. By the time he got his cigarette lit and started walking her way, she was almost entirely under the car. She slowed her movements, knowing his night vision would be wrecked because of the lighter flame and the lights at the back of the house. She managed to get completely under cover by a fraction of a second when he rounded the corner to the back of the compound.

The other man, who also smoked, looked at this guy with obvious boredom. "I'm getting tired of staying back here, when are we going to switch positions?" he asked in Arabic.

"About fifteen minutes. The night crew should be here soon. As long as those bastards didn't sleep in again."

Elle felt her tension loosen. She could use this; she just needed those idiots to move away from the back of the residence. Time was running out; the man on the patio would be done praying soon, and she would have to come up with a different approach.

The two smokers started walking. She counted on them roving together and talking for a couple of minutes. They casually walked around the corner still talking about the shortcomings of their night crew. She looked to her right and then at the man praying. He was sitting up, so she slid out from under the car and returned to a crouching position. As soon as his muscles started moving forward, she was on the move. Elle ran in an arc to try and skirt the light and stay in the shadows as much as possible. She made it to the side of the house and shifted her body toward the door.

She kept her steps light and balanced to soften any sound. Elle needed to make it inside, now, but the guard was sitting back up. She waited, frozen on the spot. He didn't move to stand but remained on his knees. As soon as he moved forward for what would likely be his last bow, she went for the door. She grabbed the knob and twisted; it opened.

A split second later, she was inside. From the schematics, she knew this room would be the kitchen, and had taken a substantial risk that no one would be there during prayer time. Her gamble paid off. The kitchen was empty, but the lights were on. She lowered herself below the window line and hugged the wall, moving fast into the hallway. She heard a man's voice. It was the target, leading his potential benefactors in prayer and the lesson following it. She placed his voice in what had appeared to be the main living room, which was at the end of the hall.

The main room of interest, on this floor, was the study, which was the door on the right before the foyer and stairs leading to the second level. Elle moved silently down the hall, pausing outside the entrance to listen for a second before peering in, quartering it a section at a time to minimize how much she exposed herself if someone was inside. It was empty. She moved into the room and looked around.

It was a medium-sized room—a large bookcase on one side and a custom-built mahogany desk in the center. A marble floor with a beautiful Persian rug which covered everything except for a two-foot gap around the walls. There were two padded chairs opposite the desk and a small couch along the far wall. Her attention turned to the bookshelf that ran the length of the room. The slight line of dust between the hard cover volumes told her they were only there for looks—to add an air of sophistication and intellect, a façade, part of negotiation tactics. Like everything else, this was all about image, not function.

Elle opened the pack attached securely to her belt and pulled out a camera. She chose one of the lower level shelves below the average person's eye line. She fastened the camera to the top portion of that shelf, making it impossible to see unless someone crouched down and looked directly at it. It also shadowed and hid the camera lens, and the books provided the perfect way to camouflage the battery pack. She knew the camera would pick up nearly the entire room. She activated and secured it.

That was easy. Perhaps too easy? Regardless, she kept moving. Returning to the study door and cautiously checked the hall. There were voices in the far room still. The Imam was still preaching. She deftly moved back into the hallway. She eased up to the foyer and checked to make sure no security lingered there. Elle felt exposed again but knew she had to proceed with caution or risk getting caught just the same.

The foyer was empty, but there was a large side table that ran along the stairwell, covered in gilded decorative plates, vases, and candleholders. It was a show piece, meant to catch the eye of anyone entering the residence to give the impression of wealth. Impulse made her go to it. She pulled out another camera, quick dry adhesive, and tape. As soon as she reached the table, she had a couple of drops of adhesive already on the camera housing and placed it under the top so that the small lens was pointing toward the door and blended in with the leg. Because the camera was fully suspended and in such a public place, it took a few extra seconds to brace with tape. This was to hold it in place until the glue bonded.

As she ran for the stairs, her eyes took in every detail, making sure the lights did not shine on the lens and reveal the camera. She also watched for movement from the main room and on the floor above. She took the stairs at a jog, landing on the balls of her feet, evenly distributing her weight to keep balance and lessen the chance of anyone hearing her footsteps on the stone. The second floor was open to the foyer, with a wide walkway that connected all the rooms. It made the residence feel large and airy, which was not conducive to her surreptitious entry. The lack of shadows or anything that could be used as concealment was very inconvenient.

As she reached the second landing, she moved to the rooms at the front of the residence and found the first one locked. She expected this type of delay at some point, and knew she was running out of time. She pulled her lock pick set out and dropped to her stomach. She paused to listen at the door and looked under the gaps near the floor.

Silence.

The room seemed empty. Elle was counting on all the guests being with the Imam. He was the most important guest, but if there were any women in the house or if any of the residents were in their rooms: game over.

She got up on one knee and worked the lock, she'd done this so many times it was second nature. It was a good thing since Tex's voice startled her. "Looks like the nightshift has arrived. Two SUVs with four men each just pulled up to the gate. They are letting them in now."

She finished the lock and sent Tex two clicks on the radio to acknowledge she got the message then opened the door to the room. Elle started a mental countdown in her head. She suspected she had approximately five minutes before the nightshift conducted their first round of the evening and before the group below was done.

This room was the master suite, and it was opulent with ornate wooden furnishings and silk pillows and gilded furniture. It was highly impressive. Elle had no doubt it was because the owner enjoyed the company of many young women and wanted them to see how rich he was, so he could entice them into bed. She assessed the room and realized that no single location would cover the space, so she opted for an angle that included the sitting area and closet. In this case, the bed was her best option.

She went to the end and lay on her back as she attached the camera to its frame. It was a large, sturdy structure, and she quickly fixed the camera and pack to it, and was on the move again. She re-entered the hall and used her tools to lock the door behind her.

As she was moving to the second room, Tex said, "Looks like two of them are going inside."

She dropped to the ground as close to the wall as she could; but kept moving forward using her knees and elbows. The guards wouldn't be able to see her from the first floor because of the angle, but she would be a sitting duck if anyone came up the stairs.

Elle reached the second bedroom when she heard the front door open and male voices speaking in Arabic. She stayed focused on her task, listened at the door, and looked under it to see if anyone occupied the space. Silence greeted her from inside, and the lights were off in the room. She paused to gauge where the security personnel were. The guards argued over the tardiness of the oncoming crew; they must have been the team supervisors. From the sound of things, they were still just inside the front door. She raised herself to one knee, watching the entire time to make certain she was not presenting an angle where they could see her. She was about to pick the lock but checked the doorknob instead. It was unlocked.

She suppressed the desire to throw the door open and race inside. The movement of the door could be seen from below, so caution was the better course of action. She inched the door open while keeping her ears tuned for any change in her environment; a pause in the guard's conversation, movement in the room, anything that indicated potential compromise.

Once the door was open just wide enough, she squeezed through and closed it with equal caution. Then, she pulled out a small flashlight with a red filter across the narrow beam of light, making it almost impossible to detect from outside the room. Compared to the master suite, this room was practically barren. The furniture was made of a very sturdy wood and had a classic design, but it was simple. A bed, dresser, nightstand, and chair with a reading lamp were all that occupied the space. This room was likely only used for unexpected company or overflow of an important guest's entourage. It didn't appear as if anyone was staying in it now, so she almost moved on. But, she'd brought a camera for each room, and since she was already there, she went with it.

She stood on the bed to get to the overhead light fixture, a very simple but elegant chandelier. She used the tools in her bag to remove the screws that held the base plate in place and pulled it free. She placed the body of the camera inside the ceiling and placed the lens in the glass decorative feature at the center of the piece. She returned to the floor and studied her work from all angles. It was good.

Elle passed her gaze over the bed and floor to be certain she didn't leave any trace of her presence and ran her hand over the duvet to smooth it from where she'd stood on the bed. Then she returned to the door. The risk would be higher now. She was out of time. At any moment the guards would make their rounds, and the prayer session would break up. She needed to move. She cracked open the door and stood listening for any tell-tale sounds that someone was approaching.

Her years of experience had served her well. She'd been in the house less than eight minutes and had already set up cameras in four rooms. But she couldn't be sure of the guards' turnover patterns. She heard the voices of the two men from earlier and estimated that they were walking down the hallway toward the kitchen. Elle darted out of the room and ran to the next bedroom that was on the other side of the stairs and sat over the rear of the residence. She was alert and controlled her foot placement, moving rapidly but silently.

She reached the third bedroom and by-passed it when the hair on the back of her neck stood on end. Something felt wrong. She went directly for the last room, the one she suspected was for the most important guests. Following the same procedures with the door, she started picking the lock. She heard the voices of the men in the main room below grow louder. Which meant the prayer session was over, and someone was leaving. She had to get inside the room before they were able to see the door from the foyer.

As soon as she was in the room, Elle locked the door. It would only buy her seconds if the Imam came back, but she needed every second she could get if the guards did a full patrol on the second floor anytime soon. She surveyed the room and was confident that this was where her target was staying. The room was opulent, similar to the master suite, but in shades of purple and gold. The bed had been turned down, and there were books and a journal on the desk near the sitting area. She used the same setup as the guest suite with the chandelier but made sure the camera angle included the desk.

Elle had just picked up the journal when she heard voices. They had to be on the landing of the second floor, and, from the sounds of it, they were moving her way. She set the journal back down and dove under the bed.

She moved to the center of the bed to take advantage of the most shadow and coverage from all angles. She had just settled when she heard a key in the lock, she froze, every sense on heightened alert. Her target—and who she assumed was a bodyguard—entered. The Imam wore a traditional dishdasha and expensive handmade leather sandals, while the man who appeared to be conducting a quick survey of the room wore tactical pants and hiking boots. She could tell by his movements that the guard was a professional and conducted the check out of habit.

Elle controlled her breathing and focused on the men. As she watched their movements, her brain calculated timing, angles of attack and escape routes if she was discovered. There was minimal conversation between the two. The guard; satisfied the room was clear, moved to the door and waited. The Imam; moved to the desk and set something on it—more books from the sound of it—and then he told the guard to wait outside. The guard acknowledged the request and left.

The Imam walked to the closet. Elle heard clothes hangers rustling. Her heart rate increased. *Shit. Is he retiring for the evening?* Voices outside the door and in the room next door drew the Imam's attention. It sounded like the occupants in the next room were arguing. She could hear a woman's voice. The woman must have been in that third bedroom the entire time.

The Imam exited the room, and she heard him berate the woman for disrespecting her husband. He called for her punishment. Silence fell. It was evident that the others had not anticipated this situation and were now at a loss of what to do. It confirmed Elle's suspicion that the occupants of the house were merely going through the motions to court a new connection they could exploit, but now they were being tested. She heard a man's shaky voice chastise his wife, and then the sound of a slap. It didn't placate the Imam. He wanted his guard to demonstrate how to punish the woman for her crimes adequately.

The woman was going to be stripped and caned.

While the household was distracted by the drama, Elle made a break for it. She slid out from under the bed and moved to the window. This would be dangerous, but she had no choice. The woman's punishment would be swift and brutal, then the Imam would return to his room. If her assessment of the situation was correct, the Iman would have the woman taken to the front of the residence and have the punishment carried out in the yard for the neighbors to watch. He would stay in the main room and watch from the safety of the window. He would want to see his influence on display but would not want to expose himself. It was her only chance, and she needed to go.

Elle approached the window at an angle to avoid casting a shadow. She parted enough of the curtain to scan the yard for the guards. Timing would be tricky here. The guards would probably move to the front, leaving only one in the rear of the residence. She needed to make sure she didn't exit while the guards were on the move and risk being in their line of sight.

Tex's voice sounded in her ear, "There's one hell of a commotion going on out front Elle. Please tell me it's not because of you."

She clicked her mic once indicating "no."

"Good, but it looks like something is going on that has everyone's attention. If you're going to do something, I would say get on with it."

She clicked twice and opened the lock on the window, then paused for a second. She didn't like having to leave the window unlocked and hoped the detail would be overlooked. Elle opened the window and moved out to balance on the four-inch ledge, finding grips on the window's edge that kept her from falling. It was a very precarious position. Closing the window, she looked around. She was currently in a thick shadow, but would have to cross in front of another window, completely exposing her in the light. From there, she would have to make her way around the residence on the ledge until she reached the overhang that covered the rear entrance. It was about fifty feet away.

Taking a deep breath to steady her nerves, she surveyed the yard below, watching closely for changes in the shadows and any sounds that told her where the security personnel were. Satisfied that it was now or never, moved along the ledge as fast as possible. Once she cleared the window, the challenge increased since she could no longer grip the frame with her hands. The side of the residence was made from a concrete-like substance. Unfortunately for her, it was in good repair.

There were very few cracks or fissures for her to use. She had to hug the wall and rely on balance to keep from falling. She moved one foot after the other, as quickly as she could, making sure to stay focused. She couldn't afford to think.

Finally, she reached the overhang and eased her weight onto it, making certain that she didn't make any sound that could draw the attention of the guard that had to be under her. She moved to the edge of the overhang and looked for him. He was completely hidden from sight. Elle knew she was running out of time. She would have to rely on memory and instinct now. She pulled a small screw out of her bag and took aim at the neighbor's residence to the east—and threw. The screw hit the window with a loud crack but did not break the pane.

As soon as she heard the sound, she was on the move. Without stopping to look where the guard was, she climbed down off of the overhang. Her gamble had worked. The guard, startled and fixated by the noise, moved to investigate. She sprinted for the same shadows that had covered her on the way into the yard then rolled under the parked cars. When Elle was under cover, she turned and looked at the guard. He was looking around the east side of the building, waiting for any other unusual sounds or activity. She needed to move again.

Climbing out from under the back of the car, keeping it between her and the guard, she gauged the wall. This part would be difficult. The wall on this side was pristine, leaving her no options for hand or toe holds. That only left her with the option of pulling herself up and over. She would have to be quick and decisive. Timing was critical.

Her heart was pounding in her chest and her breathing accelerated. She rose up behind the cars just enough to see the yard and back of the residence. The guard was by the eastern fence line, but his body language said he was no longer on alert. He was about to go back to his post. She glanced along the other side of the house to make certain the second guard hadn't returned; and made a run for it.

Elle launched herself at the wall, planting one foot on the stone face to boost herself up; she barely caught the top. She didn't allow herself to hang but pulled herself up, arms screaming in protest. Once her chest cleared the edge, she leaned across the wall and used the leverage to pivot her body until she was flat on top. Her adrenaline wanted her to continue across the wall and drop down on the other side, but her training told her to freeze.

She watched as the guard returned to his original position, and a second guard emerged from the shadows on the east side of the residence. He was directly in her sightline; but didn't show any indications that he could see her. Experience had shown that most people didn't focus on their surroundings unless something stood out; the more solid the routine, the less they observe. Freezing on top of the fence likely saved her from drawing his attention. She allowed the shadows to cloak her enough that the routine observations prevailed. She stayed on top of the fence until both guards faced away from her, then she moved over the wall.

Once she hit the ground, she navigated the trash piles, returned to where she'd left her burka, and dressed. Properly attired, she radioed Tex. "Ready to move."

"Moving, be there in five."

She waited until the five minutes had almost passed and strolled out toward the road. She got there just as Tex did, falling into step behind him as they moved back through the neighborhood the way they had come. As they passed the front of the target residence, she saw the front was lit up brightly and she could hear a woman crying. She used her peripheral vision to take in the scene as they continued walking, the woman had been whipped and was left bleeding in the front yard. It appeared that she was bound hand and foot and was to be left there for an indeterminate amount of time as punishment for her crimes against her husband. Elle felt her blood boil but she remained focused.

Soon, Number 1 would no longer be able to deliver any more acts of cruelty. She would make certain of it.

CHAPTER 9

They made it back to their vehicle with no issues. A lot of the activity in the neighborhood had died down while they were gone, but there was enough, so they could blend in. Once they were in the car, she asked, "Any issues?"

He said, "Yeah, that strawberry shisha was brutal, and I could barely stomach the juice, but this is the price we pay."

"Hey, no one said this job would be easy. Let's get moving to our next location."

Tex started the car and moved out of the dirt lot. "How did everything go on your end?"

"Not as well as I would have liked, but I got in and out clean. Tomorrow when I go back, things are going to be a little more complicated, but at least now I have the complete lay of the land and the guard's patterns."

Tex exhaled. "I know it's your show, but am I going to be anything other than your chauffeur tonight? Could I at least know what the hell you just did?"

The dejection in his voice was clear to her. "Mike, I know that you feel under-utilized, but it's not because you aren't capable. You, Eve, and Jack are at the top of your game. I just have a method, and it works for me. I've been successful because I do things differently from everyone else. Old habits die hard. Besides, all that was just prep for things to come. You'd have been bored."

Tex looked bemused. "Who are you and what have you done with Elle?"

"Suck it, Tex."

They drove the rest of the way in silence.

As they approached the second location, the scenery changed. In this part of the district, the buildings were much closer together, and in a lot of cases, the residences were stacked on top of businesses. They passed a myriad of neon and handmade signs. It was like each one was trying to be more garish than the last.

As they approached the road with the target apartment building on it, she told Tex to drive at a steady pace and watch for parking options. As they moved down the road she watched the target building and the street. The structure was sturdy and in good repair, with a café at the bottom. The building's schematics showed that the top two floors had four apartments each.

Comparing the wiring going to the target building to the ones around it, they seemed to be identical at first glance. Elle looked at each window; most were lit and looked clear of any antennas. Elle suspected that the one she was looking for had signal boosters. Since she didn't have a recent photograph or specific address for either 10 or 11, she was going to need to do a little reconnaissance to find her targets.

"I changed my mind. Drive me around to the back of the building and then I want you to go to the other apartment and start doing some recon looking for 11."

"Seriously?"

Elle sighed. She decided on the course of action before she thought about what she was doing. Tex wanted to be treated like a partner so why not. "Yes, seriously. You wanted more involvement, fine. We'll stay in contact the entire time, and you find the next target's location. You saw Eve's file on the guy. We could be in for an all-nighter waiting for his ass to return or we could luck out and catch him on the way out. One way or the other, the sooner we get eyes on the building and narrow down his apartment, the better our chances are of finding him before dawn. If you find him and have the opportunity, you need to take him out clean and quiet. Once I finish with 10, I will contact you for your location, and we'll link up. Any issues with that?"

"No issues." He drove around to the back of 10's building, and she saw the clue she was hoping for—one window had an antenna with several extra wires running to it. That was her target's apartment.

"Pull over, Tex, he's on the top floor on the north side."

Tex did what she asked and glanced up. "You sure about this? What if he's not alone in there?"

She gave him a look.

He raised his hands in surrender. "Sorry I even asked."

"Once I'm inside the building, get moving to the other apartment building. Watch for the same indicators for the apartment, and do what you can to figure out if he is inside without drawing attention to yourself. If he's not home, set up wherever you can to surveil the building until he comes back."

"Yes, Mom."

She rolled her eyes, got out of the vehicle, and moved to the back entrance.

The rear of the building had the service entrance for the café and stairs that led up to the apartments above. Elle kept in the shadows as she moved up the two flights of stairs and into the common hallway. Her target was to her left. But first she moved around the rest of the floor to check on the other apartment occupants. The apartments on the main street side of the building seemed to be occupied, and from the sounds of things, a lot of residents were watching a soccer match with some enthusiasm. The apartment directly across from her target was dark and silent.

She turned to the door of her target and listened carefully. There was no sound, but the lights were on. If her quarry was on the computer, he wouldn't be making much noise. Elle removed her knife and lock pick from her belt, set the knife on the floor, and made short work of the lock and deadbolt on the door. Putting her pick away, she grabbed her knife and inched the door open slowly, listening for any telltale squeaks or indications that the movement was noticed. Once the door was open wide enough to admit her, she entered, closed the door and turned the deadbolt.

Elle was in the open, but she still had surprise on her side. She was in a living room of sorts and knew the window with the extra wiring was down the short hall to what was likely a bedroom. The apartment was sparsely furnished with items that were miss-matched but appeared to be more about comfort and function than looks. There was a strong stench of body odor. She could see a pattern on the floor where the occupant had moved through the rooms, his feet making trails in the dust.

Elle moved in silence, quartering each doorway she came across to make certain that her target was not there. The kitchen was small, and the trash was full of bags and to-go food containers. She moved past a doorway to what would likely have been a bedroom but looked as though it was a catchall for various items and boxes.

As she approached the room in question, she heard a toilet flush and froze. The door in front of her was the bathroom. Elle weighed her options. She doubted that this man had anyone residing with him or had anyone visit in a long time. She was betting it was her target in the bathroom and that no one else was in the apartment.

Elle waited outside of the door and conjured up the image of the last known photograph of Number 10 in her mind. It was several years old, but she knew his major features would not have changed, particularly the eyes and ears. The door opened. A man walked out into the hallway. He did not see or sense her at first, but then his breath did a sharp intake as he turned. She had her target and reacted. Her hand flew with unerring accuracy between his ribs and into his heart. The blade was scalpel sharp with a lethal point and serrated edge. She didn't need to worry about blood too much; if she hit the heart just right there would be minimal blood since the heart would seize and stop pumping.

In this case, she hit her mark.

Before her target could fall, she moved in to take some of his weight to minimize the sound of his body hitting the floor. She didn't want to risk neighbors coming by to investigate loud noises. Her target was short and flabby, but not overweight, so she was able to take on most of his weight. However, dead weight can be unpredictable since it seems to bond with gravity. She stumbled under the body and barely broke their fall.

She would have some strained muscles to manage tomorrow, but it wasn't anything she hadn't experienced before. She untangled herself from the body, and finished looking around the apartment. Inside the bedroom, she found a wall of computer servers and monitors. Gambling sites on most screens, but a jihadist forum was on one. Number 10 had been monitoring a chatroom, probably preparing for tonight's propaganda. Now it was up to Jack and Eve to make sure tonight's posts were completed. Elle still had work to do.

She left the apartment as it was and returned to the door. Elle paused and listened in case anyone was in the hallway. Satisfied, she locked the door behind her and left. She returned to the street, sticking to the shadows as she moved to the next block over to meet with Tex.

"Moving, what's your location?" she asked into her radio.

Two clicks was his answer.

"Are you in the apartment building?"

Two clicks.

"Is the target apartment on the top floor?"

Two clicks.

"Have you located the target?"

One click.

"Do you need assistance?"

One click.

Damn it, she knew she had given this task to Tex, but now that it was happening, she was anxious. Her heart rate and breathing had not been affected at all while she took out her target, but now it was racing. She was worried about Tex. If anything happened to him, it would be her fault. As she walked, she forced herself to get her feelings back under control. She'd found her emotions playing a much larger role in her dealings in these last few days than she could remember happening before. But she didn't have the time or inclination to dwell on it now. She needed to be focused, and she needed to finish the job at hand.

"Copy all. Moving to an overwatch position."

Tex had the lead on this part of the mission and Elle needed to back off. His credentials made him more than qualified, and the chances were high that 11 wouldn't even be in the apartment. She steadied her breathing as she walked, and her heart rate returned to normal. She regained her focus as the building came into sight.

It was almost a carbon copy of the one she just left. The only difference was the bottom level did not have a café in it, but an empty store front that appeared to be an old video store. That gave her pause for some reason. As she approached the building, she found herself focused on the store. It had old movie posters crumbling in the windows and the remnants of shelves against the walls. It ate at her. Something wasn't right. All the hair on the back of her neck was standing on end, and her gut lurched.

"Tex, get out of the building now.

There was a pause, but then came two clicks.

She could almost hear his grumbling in the tone of the clicks.

As she stood on the street, she finally saw what she was looking for—a very small, flashing, red light. Old posters camouflaged it, but it was there. The building was rigged with explosives; she was certain of it. She looked up and saw the faint flicker of a red light on the corner of the roof, too. Number 11 was more than prepared for an assault; he was ready to go on the offensive. Typical special operations tactics had them coming in and clearing one floor at a time, and potentially fast-roping troops onto the roof. 11 was counting on that and had explosives at both points. She would wager that he kept eyes and cameras on the location to capitalize on such an occasion.

As she waited for Tex to emerge, she scanned the buildings across the street from the target. It took some time, but she found one that had a few more wires running to it. When she followed them back to their end point, she saw that they returned to the target building. Number 11 was smart and had worked to cover his tracks. She would bet anything that he pirated his own signal to make certain, if he was ever tracked, it would go to the building with the old video store instead of his actual residence. Clever.

She needed to reassess this target before they walked into another trap. She hoped that Tex hadn't made it to the bait apartment door before she called him back. A single "Arab" man walking into the building wouldn't draw attention, but if he had cameras on his door, that would be an issue. She let out her breath when she saw Tex emerge. Over the radio, she said, "On your left." His head turned, and he began to casually walk in her direction.

Once he was close enough, she could see the irritation on his face.

"What the hell, Elle, I was almost there!"

"Good, I'm glad you didn't make it since the building is rigged to blow and likely has video surveillance."

That stunned him into silence for a moment. "You sure?"

"No, I just thought it would be funny," she said.

He shifted his weight in agitation. "Sorry."

She returned her attention to the problem at hand. "11 was prepared for a raid on that building, but he would want to be close to monitor any activity there and to be able to pirate his own signal. I found some suspect cables leading to the second building on the right to the north. We need to make certain he doesn't have any other surprises waiting for us."

Tex followed her gaze to the building in question. "So, what's our next move?"

She had been pondering that herself. How much had they underestimated their opponent? Given the new information she needed to reconsider what they thought they knew about this target. He had seemed to be very conscious of his operational security, but they hadn't anticipated such a robust or extreme posture at his residence. This guy was a serious player and a psychopath considering the number of casualties he would likely cause to take out a potential raid force. Getting the video footage was all that mattered to him, and it would probably be posted on every jihadist website before the dust even cleared.

That was his weakness, the cameras. They needed to find the cameras, most importantly, the one that had the prime angle.

"We're not going to go to him. We're going to make him come to us."

"Sounds good to me. Should I just send him a written invitation?"

"Something like that. It will definitely be something that will inspire him to RSVP in person."

Elle moved until she was completely in the shadows of the apartment building across the street from the original target. Tex mirrored her movement and automatically began watching for additional threats. She scanned the area looking for the prime coverage angles for the bait building. She had no doubt that he had cameras inside the building, but there had to be ones on the outside that captured the avenues of approach to the structure, as well as the entryway. There was no way 11 wouldn't be set up to capture a dramatic entry before he switched to internal cameras. He would want to make certain that any raiding party was fully invested in the search and vulnerable to his trap when he detonated the structure. The propaganda value would be massive.

As she looked at the bait location, she saw that the lighting from her angle was perfect for capturing any activity heading into the structure. She turned, looked up, and found what she was looking for. On the far corner of the building from where she and Tex were standing was what appeared to be a small security camera, at least to the casual observer. Except it was angled to cover the bait building; and not the apartment to which it was attached.

She nudged Tex and pointed to the camera. From the angle and camera type, she was reasonably certain they were not in its field of vision, but they both pulled back into an alcove to be sure.

"That is our target camera, but we need to make sure we don't cross in another camera's field of view when we sabotage that one."

"I can shoot it out from here, but then what?" Tex asked.

Elle shook her head. "I don't want to disable it. That will likely make him suspicious and put him on alert. I want to draw him in without putting him on guard."

"How the hell are we going to do that?"

She looked around her feet and found numerous sun-bleached plastic bags and brittle paper that had gotten blown up against the building, and then trapped in the alcove they were standing in. She grabbed one of the bags and started moving to the back entrance of the building. Tex followed without question.

They reached the first floor, and she went to the apartment that had the closest windows to the camera. 11 would need regular access to the location to service his camera, but she wasn't certain if someone would be living there. As she approached the door, she signaled to Tex for silence and listened for activity. Nothing. She dropped to her knees and checked under the door and didn't see any lights. She picked the lock and opened the door, watching for wires and listening for any indications that the place was booby trapped or that someone was inside.

Elle felt a slight change in the tension on the door and stopped moving. She ran her fingers along the opening in the doorway and found what she had hoped to avoid, a tripwire. She let the door fall back closed a little to take the tension off the line. She needed to figure out what the tripwire was for before she decided how to handle it.

She turned on her last camera and used the fiber optic lens to give her a full 360 of the inside of the room, and, mainly, the tripwire.

"Give me your phone."

Tex handed her the cell. She pulled the micro SD card out of the camera and plugged it into the phone. After a moment of button crushing, she was able to review the footage with Tex looking over her shoulder.

The room was almost empty, except for a desk, a chair next to the window, and a couch in the corner, but that was it. It looked as though no one had been in the location for any lengthy amount of time. 11 was likely only using the location to access his camera system. The tripwire was attached to a strobe alarm by a hook and loop closure. Satisfied, Elle returned the phone to Tex, and went back to the doorway and unhooked the alarm.

"Watch where you place your feet. There are tracks from where this guy walks when he comes here. We need to try and avoid making any new prints that could tip him off."

Tex nodded.

They entered the apartment, and she locked the door and reset the alarm behind them. From there, she moved to the window closest to the camera and opened it carefully. The camera was about a foot away from her. She took the plastic bag and draped it in such a way that it looked like it got caught on the camera from either wind or from being dropped out the window of another apartment. It didn't completely obstruct the view of the camera, but the bag would wave in and out of the picture, consistently degrading the overall image. For someone like 11, that would be an irritation that could not be ignored. He wouldn't risk his perfect setup being marred by poor footage. Annoyed, he would come fix it as soon as he saw it. Elle suspected that he routinely monitored the camera feeds remotely. He would come before the night was over. In a way, this turn of events was a stroke of luck for her and Tex, since they had thought they'd be waiting all night for this target. Now, she doubted they would have to wait for more than an hour or two.

"We need to find a place to settle in here while we wait. 11 will be here within a couple of hours."

Tex looked a little skeptical. "That's pretty specific. You certain? I could still surveil his place, double our chances of success."

"If we put eyes on his building, he'll be alerted. Hopefully, since you didn't actually make it to the bait apartment, we didn't draw any attention already. How far in did you go? Were there other people in the building?"

"I was still on the first floor when I turned around, and yeah, it sounded like there were people in the building."

"Good, if he was watching, then, with any luck, he won't think anything of your visit. He'll come here to get the trash off his camera. When he does, we'll take him out."

She moved out of the main room and into the next adjoining room. There were lots of boxes and it smelled musty. From the amount of dust over most of the boxes, she could tell that the ones closest to the door were the most recent and the ones he still used. Opening them up, Elle found books. Lots of books: math, science, engineering, literature. Apparently, Number 11 was a self-educated psychopath. She closed the boxes and sat down with her back against the wall. She motioned for Tex to do the same.

"What's the plan, Elle?" Tex asked as he sat down.

"We wait. When he gets here, I will move to get behind him as he fixes his camera and take him out quietly. Then, we will need to move the car to the back entrance and get the body in the trunk. From there, we need to return to 10's apartment and remove that body, too. We wrap them in the tarp and go back to that trash field I pointed out earlier. The faster we get the bodies in the burn pit, the faster we get back to base."

He sat and thought for a moment.

She knew what he was going to say before he said it.

"I should take out 11. He was my task."

"We need to take him by surprise, and I'm less likely to alert him than you are. You're a big guy. If he gets even a glimpse of you, we're blown."

He was about to argue when a noise came from the hall. Her hand flew up silencing him. It was the sole of a sandal. The steps grew louder and stopped outside the door to the apartment. She removed her knife and stood up, angling her body strategically.

She heard the key in the lock and the door open— then there was a pause. The slight scraping sound told her that the alarm was being disarmed. Her heart beat and breathing were steady, yet her focus was so intense, that her vision and hearing seemed enhanced. She felt her muscles coil in anticipation as the door closed, and she heard the footsteps move to the window. Once she heard the window open, she stepped out of the room. Elle wouldn't be able to verify his identity before the kill, but she was certain this was her target or a very close associate.

She entered the main room and saw the man leaning on the desk, his full attention on removing the bag from the camera. He was small, wearing western-style clothing and had a satchel that was now on the floor at his feet. She did not hesitate. She drove her blade into the base of his skull, severing the spinal cord and killing him instantly. His body dropped onto the desk with a loud thud, but then everything was quiet again. She removed her knife and wiped off the blade on his shirt. She turned when she heard movement behind her. It was Tex. She walked around the body until she could see his face. It was in partial shadow, but based on the last known photograph of 11, there could be little doubt that this was her target.

"Time to get the car," she said.

He looked at her for a long moment before he nodded and moved to the door. "Be back in ten," he said, and he was out.

She puzzled at his reaction for a moment, then realized that for someone like Tex, taking over his task and pulling rank on him was a blow to his ego. She sighed and returned to the issue at hand. She grabbed the satchel and ruffled through the dead man's pockets.

She found a wallet, keys, cigarettes, and some pocket litter. She put it all inside the satchel with the intent of taking it back and turning it over to Eve and Jack for exploitation.

Then she found 11's tablet, which had various security camera images displayed. He had six cameras focused on the bait apartment building. She found what looked like notes for his evening posts. Those would be beneficial for Jack. She tensed when she heard footsteps in the hall but relaxed when she recognized them. Tex opened the door and slipped back inside with the tarp from the car.

The two of them moved the body onto the tarp and wrapped it up.

"The car is right outside the back entrance."

She nodded and helped Tex throw the body over his shoulder in a fireman's carry.

"Now I see why you let me come along. To do the heavy lifting."

"Aren't you always insisting you carry the heavy stuff?"

He gave her the finger.

She grabbed the satchel and held the door for him. Once he was through, she reset the alarm and locked it behind them.

They made it to the car without incident and got the body in the trunk. "Why did you reset the alarm?"

"I'm not certain if he's working with anyone else or not. We need everyone to believe that he's alive and in the wind."

They moved the car around to the back of 10's building and went inside. Elle walked into 10's apartment and past the body to his bedroom where she went to his closet and found well-worn sandals and a recently worn tracksuit. She took them and looked around the room and found a wallet and keys next to his computers. Elle grabbed them as well as a laptop in its case. By the time she was finished, Tex already had the body wrapped in a tarp, and slung over his shoulders. He waited by the door.

"There's more people in this building. You should go first to run any interference."

She nodded and went out into the hallway. Once she knew it was clear, she waved Tex out. She locked the door behind him, and then led the way out of the building. They made it to the car without issue and got the body in the trunk. She placed the laptop, and items she took from the apartment, on the rear seat floor board with the other items from 11's apartment. Then they were moving again.

They rode in silence for a couple of minutes, then Tex finally said, "Well done."

"We're not done yet. Our biggest risk of compromise is still coming. Keep your game face on. One random vehicle search and we're in for hell."

Silence returned to the car, and she sat observing the surroundings and running through scenarios in her mind. It wasn't quite eleven yet. They were running significantly ahead of schedule. There were still a few people enjoying the evening, but most had retired for the day.

She saw the bridge and the checkpoint ahead and used the mirror to check her headscarf; everything was still in place. She saw some blood on the side of Tex's neck and wiped it off. As they approached the checkpoint, they resumed their roles as a Muslim couple, and she avoided making eye contact. This time, the window went all the way down. The guard showed no interest and waved them through.

Once they were away from the lights, she chanced a look around. Everything was calm. "One last thing and then we can hightail it back to base."

"Yep, just got to drop the kids off at school, honey," he said.

She chuckled.

They drove to the field that she had pointed out earlier, and Tex followed her instructions for backing the car in near the flaming trash pit. She kept her head on a swivel as they made their approach. She knew the night had eyes. Where were those eyes? Were they sufficiently camouflaged by the trash piles to avoid raising any alarms? She stepped out of the vehicle and did a 360, measuring the angles of the refuse, and the buildings on the outskirts of the trash field.

The flames were much more subdued now, but there were still pockets of fire that hadn't turned to embers. This would be perfect for what they wanted.

Once Tex emerged from the car, she opened the trunk and retrieved one of the shovels and moved to the edge of the pit. She pushed the rubbish around creating a trench for the bodies. With Tex's help, they made a six-foot-long, three-foot-deep hole in no time. The stench was unbearable, and they both worked in silence trying not to breathe too deeply, which would likely cause them to gag or retch.

They moved with purpose. Tex grabbed one body at a time, tossing it into the trench. Elle covered them with loose trash, then moved to an area of the pit that still had open flames, grabbed a shovel full, and placed it over one body. Then they repeated the procedure for the next. The fire would spread, but it would also ensure that no one went digging through that section in hopes of finding valuables someone threw away.

As soon as they finished, they knocked as much refuse off the shovels as they could, shook off their clothes and shoes, and got back in the vehicle. By comparison, the air inside the car felt fresh like spring, and they were both glad to be in it.

"Let's get out of here, Tex."

"Yes, ma'am."

As he maneuvered out of the trash field, she watched for any movement that might indicate they had observers. All she saw was a pack of wild dogs. Once they were back on the road, she took off her headscarf, opened the window, and took some deep, cleansing breaths.

"Success?" Tex asked.

"Yeah, I would say part one was a success. Thanks for all the help. You made this a lot easier."

"Awe, shucks."

"Suck it, Tex."

She reconnected her music, and they both allowed the adrenaline to wash through them, reveling in the post-mission high.

CHAPTER 10

When they pulled back into the compound, it looked like the Special Forces guys were getting ready to roll out. That was good and bad. Good because that meant they would be preoccupied for the rest of the night and she would be able to move around the compound freely. Bad because they saw her and Tex pull in this late, in a civilian vehicle, dressed as they were, and would wonder why.

They parked outside of their building and waited. Keeping their operations out of the spotlight was key, so changing clothes before getting to the compound would have been an indicator to anybody watching the base.

"Pull off the burka and stay on my right. If they can't get a clear look at you, they may lose interest."

Elle wiggled out of the garment and got out of the car.

She and Tex moved with a determined pace and were inside their building in no time. They went to the Ops center, where Jack was typing furiously. Eve was at her desk with several open folders and taking notes off her computer screen.

Music was playing softly. "You ladies having a good night?" Elle asked.

Jack and Eve nearly jumped out of their skin.

"Oh my God, Elle, you nearly gave me a heart attack. Why are you back so soon? Did everything go okay?"

"We're fine, everything went fine. We were just able to complete what needed to be done tonight sooner than anticipated."

"I'm ready to go back to the trash pit now. What the hell am I listening to?" Tex asked.

"It's Lady Gaga and she has an amazing voice." Eve answered.

"Jack, both 10 and 11 have been out of the equation for over an hour. We've brought back some of their things for you and Eve to go through." Elle said.

"I've got it." Tex said and left to grab everything from the car.

Jack's interest was piqued. "What kind of stuff?"

"A tablet, a couple of laptops, and other items that I haven't had a chance to go through yet."

"We're on it, Elle," Eve chimed in.

"Could I ask a favor, Eve?"

"Anything, what do you need?"

"Food and a shower. Desperately. Would you walk with me to the shower and take these clothes and throw them into the laundry? I'm going to need them again tomorrow."

"Of course, that's easy. And I can get you something to eat from the galley, they should be doing mid-rats now."

Elle felt guilty asking for help with her laundry, but her adrenaline rush was fading, and she would be crashing soon.

When they reached the showers, Elle disrobed and handed her things to Eve.

"I'm glad that I have no idea what you did tonight. Otherwise, I'm not sure I could touch these."

Elle laughed. "You see? Ignorance really is bliss."

Eve shook her head and left.

After a night like this, nothing in the world felt better than a shower. Elle turned the water on as hot as she could stand and let it cascade over her back. After the initial sting on her skin, the hot water worked its magic on her sore muscles, and they started to relax. She allowed her mind to go completely blank; something rare and difficult for her, but delightful when she could manage it. She lost herself in nothing but the sensation and sound of the water for a while.

Eventually, her mind started spinning again, and she finished her shower, feeling a slight twinge of guilt over wasting water. There were rules about water conservation that were in place to ensure personnel didn't have to worry about shortages. She should have taken a combat shower, meaning she should have had the water on only long enough to get wet and then to rinse off after cleaning. Leaving the water on the entire time she was in the shower was bad form and would have drawn attention to her if anyone else had come into the trailer.

Feeling refreshed and enjoying the remains of the post-mission endorphin high, she dressed and left the trailer. As she came around the corner to head to her office, she looked over at the laundry building and froze. Eve was standing there, looking uncomfortable, but giving a polite smile to Red Shirt. He was in tactical pants and a t-shirt now, but it was definitely Red Shirt, the sociopath from the plane.

Elle should just walk away and allow Eve to extricate herself, but she approached them. "Hey! What are you doing out here? Did you forget how much work we have to do?"

A little confused, Eve said, "Sorry, I was on my way back but got caught up talking."

Elle gave her a disapproving look. "I get it. Paperwork is boring, but if we don't get it done then

we're never going to hear the end of it from the boss."
Giving Red Shirt a half smile, Elle apologized for
interrupting; and started herding Eve back to their
building.

Eve glanced over a shoulder as they walked away.
"He's staring at us. It's so creepy. Thank you."

"Do what you can to make sure you aren't alone
with that one again. He's dangerous."

"What do you mean?

"He's a sociopath."

"How do you know?"

"Takes one to know one."

Eve chuckled nervously.

She thinks I'm joking.

"What if we do see him again?"

"Eve, that guy is a full-fledged sociopath. He reeks
of violent tendencies. I'll ask Tex to go and recover my
clothes just in case he has any inclination to hang around
waiting for you to come back."

Eve stopped walking just as they reached their
office. "Oh! I forgot to get you some food. I'm so sorry,
Elle! I'll head over that way now."

Elle grabbed her arm. "Don't worry about it, Eve.
I'll ask Tex to make a round trip. He may bellyache a
little, but it'll be character building. Besides, he needs to
know about Red Shirt so he can be on the lookout, too."

"Red Shirt?" Eve asked.

"Yeah, he was on the same flight as me coming here and he was wearing a red shirt. It's as good of a nickname as any."

As they made their way back into the Ops center, Jack and Tex were working on the tablet she had brought back in 11's satchel.

When he saw her, Tex said, "You need to see this."

It was a propaganda video, and it featured Number 1 in front of the house she'd placed the cameras in earlier that evening. 11 had been there—and, he'd made a film of the woman they'd punished for disrespecting her husband. Elle's blood ran cold for a second time as she watched the Imam debase the woman at the will of Allah. This man would die, nothing would stop her.

"I want you to edit this video to give the impression that the Imam considers himself the only true voice of Allah in Daesh, and that he is beginning a power play."

"You want us to post this shit?" Tex asked incredulously.

"Seriously, Elle? This is horrible. That poor woman. How can we put this out there?" Eve asked.

Jack just sat quietly, looking sick.

Elle felt her emotions welling up. "How did you think this was going to go? That you could half-ass masquerading as these guys and post some nice chitchat in Arabic? That video was going out to a bunch of sadists regardless of whether we intervened. This way, we keep our cover, and use it so they start digging their own graves. You guys knew the deal when you signed on for the job." With that, she turned and left the room.

Sitting in her room, Elle felt unsettled. She put in her earbuds. Music usually helped clear her mind. Not now; she needed to hit something. Showered or not, she was going to the gym.

Elle changed into workout gear and grabbed some ace wraps on her way out. She heard Eve yell her name, but shot through the doors and headed to the gym without looking back. She wrapped her knuckles, put on her metal playlist; and unleashed on the heavy bag.

She felt the tension easing with each impact, and eventually she was able to work technique instead of just beating the hell out of the canvas. She eased up finally and took a step back from the bag. It was only then that she sensed she wasn't alone. She turned, and the handsome man from the day before was standing there, just a few feet away.

Elle removed her headphones. "Can I help you?"

"Your technique is good, but you telegraph your hook in your hips."

"You think so, huh?"

"I know so. For the last ten minutes, I've been watching your combinations, and I could predict your hook after the first couple of minutes. You need to work on curbing that indicator."

Elle wasn't sure what bothered her more, the fact that she had been directly observed for ten minutes without being aware, or that he was criticizing her technique. "My hook has served me well over the years, but I'll take it under advisement."

"I didn't mean any offense. Just thought I would point it out."

"What's your name?"

"Julian, yours?"

"Elle."

"Pleasure to meet you, Elle." And with that, he inclined his head to her and started to walk out of the gym.

"Leaving so soon?"

Julian turned back.

Elle's blood was still up, and Julian looked like a perfect outlet. She gestured toward the sparring mat. "Want to test out your assessment?"

"I suppose I have a few minutes."

"That sounds like you're going to take it easy on me."

"Seems only fair since I already know your moves."

"Keep telling yourself that."

Elle got some water and used a towel to wipe some of her sweat while she waited for Julian to get ready. He had hand wraps in his bag, which told her he fought regularly. He would be a challenging opponent. *Good.*

Her tension may have eased while she was working the heavy bag, but she still felt antsy, like her skin was too tight and she couldn't settle or focus. Her adrenaline was kicking up again. She wanted this fight. Julian finished wrapping his hands and moved to the center of the mat.

She followed him. "I know you team guys love to keep your hair pretty, so I'll keep it to light contact. Only minor bruising. You can tell your friends you fought off rogue ninjas."

Julian laughed, "So considerate of you. I appreciate you looking out for my fragile ego."

They circled each other. Julian's stance and footwork confirmed her suspicions; he was a well-trained fighter.

Elle feigned to her left and watched for his counter move. He didn't fall for it. She moved in and threw her jab. He dodged it and threw a counter punch that she blocked. She attacked again with a jab—cross combination that he blocked and countered. Elle intentionally telegraphed her hook and went for a body shot when Julian moved to block; it landed. She pressed her advantage by throwing another combination, landing another shot before Julian danced away from her. He was smiling.

Elle kept her body weight evenly distributed and balanced on the balls of her feet, dancing as she waited for his next attack. He came at her in a rush, throwing multiple combinations. She took several hits but returned a few of her own. Time seemed to slow down as their physical chess match continued. Her senses tunneled, and she focused on Julian. He wasn't holding back on her, and, as the fight progressed, he started landing more shots than she was. Pure muscle memory took over, and Elle captured a jab, placed her ankle behind Julian's, and swept the leg while striking his chest and pulling the trapped arm back. He hit the ground with a thud but recovered before she could use his arm to control his body.

Julian shifted, snaking his legs around her leg and hip. He grabbed her ankle, attempting to catch her in a heel hook submission. Elle spun to break the hold and wrenched her foot free as soon as the pressure eased. Lightning fast, Julian was up and on her again. He shot in low, putting his right shoulder into her torso. She sprawled her feet out, wide behind her, and wrapped her arms around his chest as she put her weight on his upper back to prevent the takedown. Her technique was solid, but her size worked against her in situations like this. Julian simply stood up with her over his shoulder like she weighed nothing.

He broke her grip from around his chest and threw her to the ground. Her breath rushed out from the impact and the sudden weight of Julian's body over hers. She caught him in a guard position, ready to keep grappling, but the second her legs wrapped around him, heat flared between them. Her training screamed at her to start "shrimping," to get out from guard and back into a fighting position, but her body wouldn't respond. The intimacy of having her legs wrapped around Julian's waist had scattered her wits. Elle's skin felt like it was on fire where he touched her, and she wanted more. Loosening her grip so she could lay back and look into his eyes, she could see that they were slightly dilated, and his breathing was ragged. He felt it, too.

He must have read the desire in her eyes too because the next thing she knew, he pinned her wrists to the mat above her head and kissed her. Elle felt the impact of the kiss throughout her entire body. She felt weak and powerful at the same time. Julian deepened the kiss as he ran one hand down her arm, grazing the side of her breast and coming to rest on her hip. He gripped her hard and pulled her body in tight. Elle could feel how hard he was, and it sent her body into overdrive. She took advantage of his unsteady position and rolled him over onto his back. As she straddled him, Julian sat up and kissed her again, more passionately this time. Elle rubbed herself against him shamelessly in a vain attempt to douse the fire that was consuming her entire body. She felt branded by his touch as he explored her body with his hands. All rational thought disappeared; time stopped.

A door slammed shut at the front of the gym and reality came crashing in. Julian pulled back. Elle moved off his lap, even though her body was literally trembling with desire. They sat and looked at each other for a while, both trying to regain control of themselves. Elle didn't want this to end, but any other option right now was insane.

"Thanks for the fight. I withdraw my critique about your hook," Julian said.

Elle burst out with a laugh. "You're welcome."

"Round two?"

She started to say no but reconsidered. "No promises."

Julian got to his feet and held out his hand. She took it, and he pulled her up and against him.

"Until next time." He leaned in and kissed her again before he released her and gathered his things.

Elle watched as he walked out, a little stunned but mostly thrilled. She took a few deep breaths. At least she finally felt better. She pulled off the wraps and gathered her things.

The gym was quiet again, so she stayed for a while to cool down her muscles and stretch before she made her way back to the office.

Pushing Julian from her mind was difficult. But once she started war-gaming her plan, working out the details of what was to come, she fell back into a familiar groove.

She walked back to her building and went directly to her room. Eve was sitting on her bed. There was a container of food from the chow hall, and her suit was hanging to dry. Elle's first reaction was irritation that Eve had done this regardless of her warning about Red Shirt, but she stamped down on that and refocused herself. Eve was an adult, and she could make her own decisions.

"Elle, I'm sorry. We all are, about earlier, and we are standing by to support you no matter what."

"I appreciate that Eve, and for the food and getting my suit."

"Tex did that. I think we'll have the video ready for your approval within the next hour."

"Thank you. Let me know when the video's ready."

Eve left.

Elle dug into her plate. She needed another shower, but right now, she needed food more.

By the time she got back from showering, the video was ready for her review.

While the material was the same, the whole effect was different. Jack had done an excellent job of editing the video and cutting away to the footage of the woman's punishment when he needed to manipulate the sound. Anyone seeing it would get the feeling that

135

the Iman was trying to maneuver himself into power. It was chilling.

"Excellent work, Jack. Get it uploaded as soon as possible. Any updates from the materials we brought back?"

"So far, it looks like we have current footage of most of our target list and a host of associates we still need to identify. We'll pull still images from this. We also have IP and MAC addresses as well as IMEI and SIM data and some email communications that make it sound like the Daesh clerics had differing opinions on which Imams were delivering the proper messages for the group. I've updated your folders and will keep digging."

Elle nodded and moved to her desk to retrieve the folders. "Tex, I want to be on the road again at the same time tonight. Only one location, though, and then straight back. Be ready for another stop at that vehicle checkpoint. Eve, check the current intel. Make sure the rest of the route is still clear and nothing has changed in the Karada District. Jack, keep posting as 10 and 11, and let me know if anything unusual comes up. Make sure you sign off when they normally would and get some sleep. I want you up at least two hours before Tex and I leave to check the status of everything and note the reactions to the video."

She left them to their assignments and walked back to her room. She felt exhausted. As she laid in the darkness, she went over the plans for that evening's mission until she felt confident, then tried to shut off her thoughts to go to sleep. But as she started to drift off, her mind wandered back to Julian. *Damn.* She had to use a meditation technique to clear her mind. A little while later, she fell into a dreamless sleep.

CHAPTER 11

Elle woke up focused and feeling more like herself. She stretched and grabbed her toiletries to make the trek to the bathroom. As she walked through the building, it was quiet. The Ops center was empty, so her team was likely still asleep.

Pop-Tarts or Clif Bars would suit her fine for breakfast, so she went to the kitchen to grab food and make some coffee.

"Morning Elle," Tex greeted as he walked in.

Elle nodded and noted he seemed extra perky.

She took her breakfast and went to the Ops center and sat at her desk to eat and wait for an update from her team.

Jack was in his chair typing incessantly.

Tex sat at his desk and kicked his feet up as he turned on the monitor that showed the news. The headline was about the latest propaganda video from the

Islamic State. The footage was creating all the shockwaves she had anticipated—the power shift had been picked up on.

Several so-called experts the reporters interviewed gave their opinions about what this video could mean about the inner workings of the group. Elle turned to Jack who had stopped typing and was watching the report intently. She could tell that he was stunned to see the reaction that his work had caused.

"Excellent work, Jack. This is exactly what I was hoping for. Have there been any angry messages to the hackers?"

"Yeah, you could say that. There are messages that are everything from confusion to pissed." Jack replied.

"Do you have any identities? Any leads on who's most incensed?" Elle inquired.

"Not yet, but soon."

"Any indication that Number 1 has seen the video and reacted?" Elle asked.

"Some of the messages seem to be trying to understand what happened with the editing, but nothing direct," Jack said.

"Keep me posted. Tex, are we all set for tonight?"

"Got the car set up before I hit the rack. We're ready."

Eve walked in and handed Elle a folder. "Before I went to sleep I put this together. It appears there are sects within Daesh. The Imams and Clerics seem to be at odds and their divides are showing. It's almost like a high school drama. The popular kids are disagreeing, so all the minions are taking sides. It's ridiculous, but it may be something."

Elle took a glance inside the folder. It looked like the guys in Syria, and the guys in Iraq were not on the same page with the future of the group's spiritual basis. "Tex, we're going to step off at 1930, be ready. Jack, keep working the sites and find me the identities of the people who are reacting to the video. Eve, good work, please give me a rundown of the intelligence picture at 1900. I'll be in the shop or in my room if anything comes up."

The hours passed quickly. Elle was holstering her pistol when Tex walked into her room.

"Thought this was going to be another quiet in and out?"

"Given that this is the second time going into this location, the risk for something going wrong is higher. While a shootout would be last resort, better to be safe...."

He nodded. "We're ready for you in the Ops center."

She walked in, and perched on a desk.

Jack cleared his throat. "I was able to determine that the Imam was one of the profiles confused by the tone of the video. His messages come across as being flattered by the portrayal but worried that too much focus was placed on him. It looks like you were right about the guy. The biggest win, though, was I think I've identified a profile being used by al-Baghdadi, or at least someone very close to him. Those messages are angry. I followed them to multiple recipients demanding an explanation for the video. One of the messages is going to Number 1, reminding him of his place. They never identify themselves, but if I had to guess, the author of those messages is the top bad guy himself."

"Good, we're getting the right amount of attention. When we get back tonight, I need you ready to make another video. I'll be bringing back lots of footage, so be prepared to scan for Number 1 and any interactions he had. Time will be critical. Whatever support you need, figure it out now, and get set up so we can hit it hard."

"I'll be ready. I've got some new software that I think will be perfect."

Elle turned her attention to Eve. "What do you have for me?"

Eve pulled up PowerPoint slides on the monitor behind her and started with a rundown of the latest intelligence being reported in the area. "The topic of the day has been that new video from Imam Khalid Omar—I mean Number 1. I haven't seen anything that indicates awareness of the fact that two of their own are missing or that their communications have been compromised. We were able to get several internet profiles and telephone numbers that have connections to various members of the group. However, they seem to be disposable, so we're looking for any patterns or possible weaknesses we can use to get more information. There have been no indications that the Imam has any intention of cutting his trip short."

Eve moved through the rest of her slides with each new point.

"Last night, the Special Ops team here attempted to acquire a courier they believe is directly connected with the Daesh leadership, but unfortunately it was a dry hole. Tonight, they have a capture-kill mission in Wasser al Salam so they'll be west of Baghdad. Significant activity shows heightened tensions in Sadr City and the Shullah district, but this is likely sectarian in nature. The route to your target location is assessed to be clear. Weather will be clear. Illumination is the same as last night until around midnight, and then the potential for sandstorms will increase due to a change in the winds."

"Good, Eve, no questions. I want you ready to help Jack when we get back, and keep tabs on any changes to the threat reporting. Tex, grab your gear and be ready to leave in fifteen. Evening prayer is at 2038, and I intend to take advantage of every minute I can."

Tex made an affronted gesture and struck a pose. "Don't I look ready? This is my Tuesday night in Baghdad best."

Elle fought a smile. "Maybe you should go with a pink shirt next time. It seems more you."

Tex gave her the finger. "Seriously, Elle, I'm ready. Any thoughts on the checkpoints?"

She had been thinking about that. "We can't count on a guard change, so I would anticipate worse-case scenarios. First, it's the same guys. Second, it's a group that's amped up. You seemed to have built rapport with the guy last night. Try to use that to your advantage. If it's a suspicious group, we're going to have to be creative. I'll take your lead unless I see something that can be of use. But, do what you can to read the scene and get on their good side."

"Easy day. Everyone loves me," he replied. "Can I choose the music selection this time?"

"Not a chance in hell. I bet your iPod's riddled with boy bands and Britney Spears. I just can't handle that kind of torture."

After a good laugh, everyone got back to work.

Elle could tell Eve wanted to say something to her, and that her team was making an effort to get everything back to normal. They were worried that the team dynamic was permanently damaged. Truthfully, she didn't know if it had been. Their reactions to seeing the dark side of what she did had changed things. And, the long-term ramifications had so many variables it was impossible to predict how things would develop. So, she refused to dwell on it or invite a return to the emotional onslaught.

As they departed the office, she saw that the compound was full of activity. The operators were getting ready to leave on a mission of their own. It could potentially help her. The base had to have eyes and ears reporting activity to anyone willing to pay for it. If any hint got out of where these guys were going tonight, that would put her target at ease and security wouldn't be anticipating a raid.

They got into the vehicle and were on their way within seconds, drawing only passing glances. Elle turned on her music and put on her headscarf. She sat quietly and just watched the surroundings as she mentally prepared for what was to come.

"Elle, can I ask you something?"

The tone of his voice put her on guard. "Sure."

"I saw your face when Eve gave the real name for our target tonight. Why do you have an issue with it? Why the numbers?"

Elle didn't answer, so Tex kept throwing glances her way.

Finally, she said, "Because it's the job and you don't make it personal."

"But these are horrible people, if you can even call them that. And I know you don't have any issue with killing. So, why the restriction?"

"Taking a life will leave a mark on you no matter the circumstances, if you allow it to have any personal associations. The numbers are just tasks to be completed to get to an end goal. Tonight, I go after another Number 1. There have been others. They had names, families, and if I put any thought into it I could tell you who they were, but I don't want to do that. They are just numbers in various jobs over the years, and I have absolutely no personal connection to them. So, they are easily forgotten."

They returned to silence, and she could see that Tex was deep in thought. It stayed that way until they came to the checkpoint into the Karada District. When they got to the checkpoint, they saw the same crew from the previous evening. The guard didn't even bat an eye at Tex, just smiled and waved him through with a few pleasantries.

Before she knew it, they were back at the market and moving through the streets toward her target. They followed the same procedure from the previous night, and she quickly moved into the alley and placed her burka in the alcove.

When she got to the wall behind the property, she eased herself to the top to get a look at the layout. Call to prayer was still a few minutes away, and she needed to decide on whether to continue onto the property or wait in the shadows. As she cautiously climbed and looked over the wall, she was not happy with what she saw. There were four guards in the back instead of two, double from the last time. She cursed under her breath. Matters were about to get complicated.

The video had made Number 1's hosts nervous, and they brought in additional security to protect their interests until more information became available. Time would not be on her side tonight; she needed to gather information as quickly as possible to navigate the residence. She calculated the guard's demeanor and body language, as well as their positions on the property. They were vigilant but not expectant. She would need to consider other options.

Her eyes scanned the residence and noticed that the office window on the lower level was partially open. At first, she was surprised by the carelessness, but then she saw a shadow cross the window and realized that the room was occupied. With the amount of guards outside, the inhabitants wouldn't think twice about allowing some fresh air into the room. The question then became: would they remember to close it when call to prayer sounded or would their arrogance prevail? She couldn't count on it, but she planned her approach as if that option remained available. She would need to be quick and decisive; the risk would be high but it was doable. She continued to look for other avenues to gain entry into the house. When call to prayer sounded, it was time to move.

The guards in the back broke off into pairs, two went to pray, and the other two took opposing sides of the house to begin a roving patrol. *Shit.* If the guards in the front were doing the same, then there would be overlapping patrols. Any gaps in coverage would be almost nonexistent. She needed to move. The longer she stayed, the shorter any window would be. She climbed over the wall and dropped below the parked cars. She watched the roving patrol and briefly considered shadowing them, but the shadows were not deep enough for her to be able to avoid being seen. She looked up to the second deck and thought about the window she had left open the previous night. Had they found it and secured it?

It was her best option, even with the uncertainties. Not to mention, it would force her to move around inside the house more. She had wanted to use the same route as the previous night for maximum efficiency. Once she saw an opening, she took it and moved across the yard. Tonight, speed took precedence over stealth. She made it to the corner of the residence and paused to check on the guard's progress. She caught movement out of the corner of her eye and saw the roving patrol making his way toward her. She angled her body to give herself as much cover as possible and started to climb.

Senses on high alert, breathing even and controlled, Elle climbed to the top of the overhang above the patio and lay prone. She heard the steady footsteps of the roving guard; he hadn't seen her. When he got to the back of the house, he stopped moving. Now, it was a waiting game. Elle was visible, and time was flying by, but she couldn't move, or it would draw attention.

She strained her ears for any telltale sign that the guards had been alerted to something amiss, but she didn't hear anything unusual. The mind could do horrible things in situations like this if you let your imagination run free. But, she refused to allow her mind to drift and stayed focused on the guard's movement below, knowing she would need to move as soon as possible. If there was a roving guard checking the windows on the second floor, she would be spotted easily, but this was her only option.

After several long minutes, she heard footsteps moving away from her position, and she chanced a look to verify that the guard was leaving. He was. She got to her feet; and returned to climbing to the second floor. The timing on this had to be perfect. For this to work, Elle had to essentially shadow the roving guard as she moved to the window on the second floor. It was the only chance she had to get to the window before the other guard would spot her. Since movement drew the eye, she was counting on the guard on the ground giving her a few extra seconds by pulling focus to him.

As she approached the window, she saw that the lights were out, which was good for her as long as no one was in the room. She glanced down at the roving patrol and could see the approaching guard from the front. Her window of opportunity was almost closed. It was now or never. She lifted the window, and it moved freely. She poured herself in smoothly.

Once inside, she stayed still and listened. No sound of alarm, no quickened footsteps or any indication she had been detected. Very slowly, she closed the window, watching to see if the guards slowed or turned their heads in her direction. Once shut, she was on the move again. She pulled her flashlight and did a quick scan of the room. Number 1's suitcase was out and partially packed. It looked like he was planning on leaving in the morning. Good thing she hadn't delayed returning; her target may have been more nervous about the strange change of events than she had predicted.

Elle moved to the door and decided on her best course of action. She would retrieve the cameras the way she'd installed them, starting on the first floor and working her way back upstairs. She listened at the door then moved, risking leaving the door unlocked to facilitate her return. She ran through the upper level, relying on her senses to alert her of danger. It was a gamble, but speed was essential here. She had to retrieve all the cameras and get back into the target bedroom before prayer time was over. She couldn't count on another distraction to help her.

Elle flew through the residence, deftly placing her feet to ensure silence as well as speed. Entering the foyer, she heard voices coming from the kitchen and put on a burst of speed to get to the office. It was a brazen action, but her luck held as she entered and found it empty. The light was on, though, so she dropped to the ground to avoid casting a shadow that could draw the guard to the open window. She crawled to the bookcase and retrieved her camera. Just as she finished putting it in her bag, she heard approaching voices. She crawled to the desk and hid. If the guards came in and did a search, she would have to fight her way out, and the mission would be blown.

She heard two men enter the room, and she tensed when one cursed. She moved her hand to her holster and started to pull her pistol. Elle held her position, muscles coiled and ready to attack. One of the guards crossed the room to the window, leaned out, and yelled at what had to have been the roving patrol. He was chastising them for not reporting an open window, calling them incompetent, blind, and some other choice phrases. He slammed the window shut, locked it, and pulled the curtain with one last obscene gesture to the man outside.

Both men left the room. And, from the sound of things, their intent was to continue the conversation with the roving patrol outside. She held her position until she heard the front door open and then she was on the move. Staying low, she headed back into the foyer to retrieve the camera under the table—seconds later she bound back up the stairs to the bedrooms. She was in and out of each of the rooms with her cameras and heading back to the target suite in minutes.

Now, it was another waiting game. Given the partially packed suitcase, she anticipated Number 1 would be calling it an early night. He wouldn't want to tempt anymore unforeseen fireworks. One way or the other, though, she would wait for as long as she had to. She took the time to study the room and refine her final approach and escape. Periodically, she stretched to keep her blood flowing, and her muscles relaxed. There was no anticipation or anxiety about things to come, just calculated purpose. She was a weapon, neither good nor bad—one with a job to perform.

Eventually, she heard voices from below then footsteps on the stairs. It was time. She pulled her knife and returned to her hiding spot from the night before, under the bed. The door opened, and the light turned on. As before, the bodyguard entered the room and did a quick assessment. The target was not a patient man and sent the bodyguard away gruffly. Neither man had any inclination that the bedroom wasn't safe.

Number 1 moved to the dresser and pulled out a nightshirt. He threw it on the bed and then changed his clothes. Once that was done, he sat at his desk and wrote in his journal for a while. A knock on the door startled both him and Elle, and the target shouted that he did not want to be disturbed. It was the bodyguard with tea. Her target sighed audibly and went to the door to retrieve the beverage. He didn't even thank the man— just shut the door in his face.

Her target returned to the desk and his writing, occasionally sipping his tea. She bided her time; she couldn't risk impatience now. Eventually, Number 1 finished his drink and turned off the light before getting into bed. She focused in on his breathing and waited until it was even and slow. The wait also allowed her eyes time to adjust to the dark room. She already had the layout memorized so she knew she could maneuver around without error.

Once she was certain that he was asleep, she eased out from under the bed. She did not hesitate. She angled herself to avoid the blood spray, covered his mouth, and brutally slit his throat. Even in the dark of the room, she detected the motion of the blood, and the smell of copper was impossible to miss. She kept her hand pressed across the target's mouth on the off chance he was capable of making a sound. She held him in place while he feebly attempted to stifle the blood flow. She had severed his arteries; he would bleed out in a minute or two.

After a few moments, it was over. The target was dead, the body already starting to cool with the loss of blood. Elle had to finish what needed to be done and get out of the residence. Using her flashlight, she opened the dead man's mouth and cut out his tongue. It was vile work, but she did not allow her mind to dwell on the reality of what she was doing. It was just another task. She pulled a pillow from the bed and moved it to the base of the door to block any light from showing out into the hallway. She couldn't risk the bodyguard wondering why his charge was awake and check on him.

She turned on the light to the horror movie she'd created. Retrieving her camera, she filmed some close shots of the corpse, and then turned the lights back off. She was done here, and it was time to go. Switching off the lights and moving to the window, she looked for the roving patrol. Her intention was to depart the same way she entered, but she didn't see either man. That meant they were paused in their rove at the front and back of the house.

Her skin started to crawl and instinct told her to get moving. She didn't question it. She opened the window and shot out onto the ledge. Her heart rate jumped and her body urged her to run. She trusted her gut and moved along the ledge as fast as possible. She was about to round the corner when she saw a light out of the corner of her eye. Someone had entered the target room. She had a fraction of a second to whip around the corner and blend into the shadows. All hell was about to break loose.

And then came the alarm. The men below started to fan out around the residence, all on high alert. She dropped to the patio cover, and crawled to the edge. It was only a matter of time before the search inside would move to the grounds. She rolled onto her back; so that she could pull her pistol and suppressor simultaneously. Muscle memory took over; she fit them together efficiently. She took a breath and launched into action.

Using one hand to brace herself on a support post, she swung her upper body so that she was half hanging upside down from the roof. The two guards at the back of the house were scanning the compound, and one faced her. His eyes widened in surprise just as she shot him between the eyes. His head snapped back from the impact of the bullet, and, before he could even start to fall, she was sighting in on the second man. Since suppressors didn't truly silence gunshots, he had started to turn toward the sound. She shot him in the head, right above his ear.

Still using the post as a brace, Elle swung the rest of her body over the roof and fell to the ground. She absorbed the shock, allowing her knees to buckle her into a roll. This time, Elle followed through with the action and was up and running across the compound at top speed. She bounded up the wall and pulled herself over. She did not pause at the top but allowed a glance back just before she dropped to the other side. The roving patrols were returning, in a manner of seconds, the bodies of the other guards would be found, and the search would expand past the compound.

She ran through the alley as fast as she could while still placing her feet to avoid falling or making too much noise. Renewed shouts of alarm chased her. She made it to the alcove where she left her disguise and threw it on. As soon as her scarf was in place, she walked casually toward the café.

She got on her radio. "Tex, I'm heading your way, I need you to meet me in front of the café."

Tex responded, "Copy all. It looks like quite the party has started back there. The place is lit up like the Fourth of July."

That wasn't good. Elle could only hope that they were still clearing the compound, which would give her the few minutes she needed to get to Tex before they started checking the alley and streets. She saw the café ahead and the towering figure of her teammate exiting. He stretched and checked his watch, giving every appearance of being at ease. When he saw her approach, he walked over and said in Arabic loud enough for those who were close to hear, "I'm ready to go now."

She allowed herself to smile behind the scarf as she fell in step behind him. Tex played to the crowd, and it worked. The men who had been watching her approach were suddenly no longer interested and returned their attention to the disturbance down the road. She was just another man's wife, waiting for him to take the lead. They all assumed that she had been waiting patiently for him and had come at his bidding.

Once they were out of earshot, she told Tex, "Be prepared to be questioned when we walk by. Hopefully, we will just look like people trying to get a closer look at the commotion, but in case they're being thorough you'll need to be ready."

"Why don't we just walk around to another street?"

"They'll pay the most attention to people looking like they are trying to avoid being seen. No one expects someone who has just fled to come back. If we just walk by and act like we're passing through, the most likely scenario is that they'll ask whether we saw anyone running away."

Tex nodded and squared his shoulders, ready to get into character if need be. As they neared the target residence, two men stood at the main gate. One talked on a radio. It sounded like he was directing the search—men were in the alley now. As they approached, the second man watched them intently. Elle kept her eyes down and walked along behind Tex like a good wife. Tex kept the pace, but she could tell from his gait he was taking in the spectacle.

When they were almost directly across from the residence, the second man called out, "Stop!"

Tex paused and turned toward the man, who walked across the street toward them.

Elle stayed behind Tex slightly to his left.

The man glanced at her and returned his attention to Tex. "Where are you coming from?"

"The café. Is there a problem?"

"That's not your concern. Have you seen anything suspicious or anyone else out on the street?" the man continued.

"No. Are we in danger here?" Tex asked.

The man didn't even acknowledge the question. He shifted his attention to Elle and asked, "What about you? What did you see?"

She shrank into herself shaking her head, and, right on cue, Tex snapped his fingers at her and directed her to stand behind him. She obeyed. Tex then addressed the man indignantly.

"Please do not speak to my wife. If she had seen anything suspicious, she would have told me immediately."

The man debated, then said, "Fine, be on your way." And he turned back toward the residence.

She and Tex continued to their car and did not speak again until they were past the bridge checkpoint. She laid her head back against the seat and took several deep breaths. Tonight, hadn't gone as planned, but it was done. She was one step closer to finishing and moving to the next phase.

Unaware of exactly how far off the situation had gone, but completely aware of her demeanor, Tex asked, "Things get a little exciting tonight?"

She snorted.

He smiled and feigned innocent inquiry.

Elle rolled her eyes. "Oh, no, it was totally standard, nothing of interest at all."

Tex kept going with the jokes. "You know if you keep slacking off and taking the easy jobs, you're going to get bored. Where's your sense of adventure?"

"Hmm, good point." Elle felt herself relaxing.

They fell into a comfortable silence for a while, and the miles passed by quickly. Tex didn't press her for any details about what had happened. It seemed that they had returned to the previous balance in their relationship. She wondered if it would last. As they reached the compound, she cleared her head for the next task. It was going to be tedious work, but they needed to get through all the video footage to design their next propaganda film. Elle knew that at least some of the video footage would be jarring for the team, but she couldn't do it all herself and stay on schedule.

It would be a test of their commitment to the job.

CHAPTER 12

As they got out of the car, the compound appeared vacant. All the operators must still be involved in their mission. They walked into their building and went straight to the Ops center. Both Eve and Jack were there working. Their heads shot up when they heard them enter.

Elle didn't miss the relief in Eve's eyes. "I'm so glad you made it back okay. There's a lot of activity around that neighborhood now. So far, no one is saying why, but there's a lot of speculation about a break in targeting a wealthy businessman."

Elle turned to Jack. "Anything on our hijacked websites?"

He shook his head. "Everyone is still talking about the video from last night. They don't seem to have any idea that anything else is going on."

"How are those discussions going?"

"Good, as far as I can tell. I've been doing what I can to sow the seeds of distrust, and I think it's working. It's not really my forte, but I think it's made enough people question what they know. The discussions are gaining steam."

Jack's smug look told her more than his words. He was proud of his work and was even enjoying messing with the terrorist sympathizers.

"Excellent, we're about to give it one hell of a push." She took off her bag, pulled out all the cameras, and put them on his desk. "Do you have everything ready for these?"

"Yeah, I've got my equipment set up to catalog all of the footage, a program that will index any images with movement, and then another that will mark audio that's usable in my editing software. How many cameras did you use?"

"Five."

"Okay, five cameras running for about twenty-four hours...I'll need about two hours to run them through the program. Then I can give you a better idea of how long it will take to view them."

"Let's get it done. Time is critical here. They haven't announced that Number 1 is dead yet, so they must be in cover-their-ass mode right now. Someone will have to say something soon, though. We want our next video to emerge first. If not, then we'll have to present it differently. What support do you need?"

"I've got this part, really just takes one person. But after that, if we could each take a video, it will go a lot faster. The indexing will help us shoot through to the spots of most interest." Jack replied.

Elle nodded. "Get yourselves ready to dig in for as long as it takes. I'm going to get cleaned up and grab food and coffee," she said to Eve and Tex.

Tex nodded.

Eve nodded and said, "I've got a pot of coffee going already, and some Mountain Dew for you, Jack."

Jack smiled and gave a her a hearty thanks, blushing a little. Sometimes, he really was a walking stereotype for a computer nerd.

Elle went straight to their shop and pulled out her pistol and suppressor. She was cleaning her pistol when she felt eyes on her and looked up to see Tex.

He did not miss the significance of the fact that she was cleaning her gun. "You need anything?"

She studied him for a moment. "No thanks, I've got this."

He nodded.

As he started to walk away, she added, "But you should definitely rethink your wardrobe. You look like a middle eastern gigolo."

"Ha! You're just jealous because I make this shit look good."

Once she was finished with her pistol, she showered and made a round trip to the chow hall. The building was a massive structure covered by a concrete barrier to prevent mortar rounds from landing in the middle of a bunch of people having a meal. It could hold around two hundred people, but right now it was being operated by a skeleton crew—just a few people to keep things tidy and to refresh the food they kept out for people to grab and go. She grabbed a Styrofoam container and filled it. Then, she stopped by the beverage cooler and grabbed a Gatorade and a Rip-it. She'd need the electrolytes and the energy boost tonight. She returned to their building and went to her room to have some time alone.

Over the years, she'd found that time to herself was almost as important to her mental readiness as research. Being around people was draining. Elle didn't mind people, but it always felt like she was assessing things and then performing, constantly evaluating and adjusting to fit in with the situation. It was instinct, and it took her a while to admit that she couldn't turn it off.

Where some people thrived on social interaction, she was often exhausted by it. Elle needed time to herself to recharge her endurance. She sat in her room, put on her headphones and ate. She allowed her mind to clear and zone into the music. As she finished her meal, she started to bring herself out of her little reprieve. She could tell time had passed and checked her watch. It had been a couple of hours since she left her team.

When she walked into the Ops center, Jack was buzzing with energy and working off several monitors all at once. Eve and Tex were at their desks watching Jack with bemused expressions. No one noticed her.

"We ready, Jack?" she asked.

Jack jumped, smiled, and started talking rapidly, "We are very ready. My software worked perfectly from what I can tell, and we cut our video viewing time by almost two thirds. If we break everything up between us, I think we can scan through all the indexed footage in about eight hours."

"We need to triage faster than that for this next phase. I need everyone looking for a scene that could be manipulated to be the target discussing mutiny. Scan for any footage with our target in it, mark it, and make another note for any footage with body language that will help sell the scene. We'll keep all the footage for additional use later, but this next part is specific and needs to happen in the next few hours. Once we have that, Jack, I need you to put together a masterpiece that makes it sound like the target had proof that the leaders of Daesh were betraying the group and using their power for their own gain. Make it sound like he had information that they weren't true Muslims and that he was going to come forward with evidence. I imagine most of his interactions will give you enough rhetoric to be manipulated into what we want fairly easily. This guy loved himself and railed about the imperfections of others, a few words changed here and there, and we will completely change the overall meaning to meet our goal. We need the video to get posted as soon as possible so we can take full advantage of the coming chaos from the target's death."

"I can definitely do that," Jack stated with confidence. He turned to his monitor and pulled up several files that he then divided on the monitors on the wall. "Everyone get comfortable. I'll increase the playback speed of all the clips by a third. As soon as you see something of note, call it out and we'll focus in on it to see if it meets the criteria. While that's going on, I'll start taking his public speeches and putting them into my editing software. Once we have a workable clip, we'll take whatever is usable in the audio to add to the illusion that it happened recently."

Eve and Tex pulled up chairs and claimed screens. Elle joined them and took the remaining monitors. Numerous scenes had the target in them, but they proved to be either him alone in his room or holding court with various people and not suitable for the scene they were creating. Having so many people involved made it too easy for the footage to be discredited since the number of "witnesses" to the actual event would support each other's claims that the video was faked. A one-on-one conversation would be significantly harder to discredit. The hours passed slowly as they scoured the footage. Elle started to war game her next move if the videos proved inadequate.

"Look at this!" Jack brought up Eve's screen on the main monitor, and they all watched as the target was invited by another man to take a seat in the office. He excused his bodyguard, and the two of them sat discussing the target's next move. It quickly became clear that the discussion had been prompted by the previous video, and the other man in the scene was concerned about the fallout.

The target was as arrogant and self-righteous as Elle had predicted. He truly believed that he was smarter and better than others. He stated it openly. And from what the target was saying, it would only take a few modifications to make this footage work. The other man was anxious, and he went so far to suggest that violence was likely to follow. The scene was perfect.

"I think the other man is the owner of the house. He must have seen the video incident as a power play, and he was trying to navigate through dangerous ground. He would have hated not knowing who held the power. It would make it impossible for him to predict who he should be cozying up to. He'd have been terrified that he was housing the loser and be seen as aiding the enemy by the winner," Eve said.

Elle smiled and looked at Jack. "This is perfect. Start working your magic. As soon as it's ready, let me know. How much time do you think you'll need?"

"Got a lot to work with here, so I think I can have something ready in about an hour."

She turned to Eve and Tex. "Eve, help Jack when you can, and try to keep him sane. Once we get the video uploaded, I want him to get some sleep. He's bound to crash from all the caffeine and sugar soon, anyway. This new video is going to create serious shock waves. He needs to nap while he can. Things are about to blow up on those websites."

"I'm sitting right here, Elle. I can hear you and I'm not a child," Jack said.

"Really? Did you finally hit puberty?"

Jack grumbled some curse words but went back to working without further protest.

Elle returned her attention to Eve. "Also, tomorrow night I'm off to Al Qaim for Number 8. I'll need any updates available and a pre-mission brief by 1800. Tex, we still good with the helo and snipers?"

"Yeah, they will be ready to go. Wheels up by 1830 from the far helo pad. We're still going to draw a lot of attention—but at least using the far pad, no one will get a good look at us. Got you a pilot, co-pilot, two shooters, and I'll be there to keep everyone in check while you're gone. All have signed nondisclosure agreements. And, understand that it's a black op that they do not have a need-to-know for."

Elle nodded. "We'll brief them in the air. The less they know the better. I'll be fast-roping in, so I'll need a spot outside the city to get dropped off, and then I'll proceed on foot. You will take the helo to a standoff location to wait for my signal. If everything goes perfectly, I'll call for an extract at the pickup site, and you guys will just come in and scoop me up. If things get hot, well, that's what the snipers are for. I'll need you running that part of the op."

Tex smiled. "Ah, yes, babysitting operators, my favorite pastime. I suppose I should pack some games and snacks and maybe some crayons."

"Doubt they've learned to color inside the lines, so you might want to go with finger paints," Elle retorted. "I don't need a bunch of cowboys messing anything up. I'm counting on you to keep them in line. They're supposed to be the failsafe. I don't need them becoming the problem."

"I've got you. I'll make sure they stick to the job," Tex said.

"I'll have the best infil and exfil locations for you before your brief tonight," Eve added. "Did you need anything else?"

"That should do it. When Tex and I return tomorrow, we will do a final assessment of where we stand. And then it's lights out for all of us. Friday morning, we pack up and get out of here. Jack, be prepared to take your borrowed internet personas on the road. They're going to keep posting from a 'self-imposed' exile."

Jack looked intrigued. "That's going to take some creative routing and IP masking—that should be interesting."

"Glad to make you happy, dear. I'll be prepping my gear for tomorrow. Call me when the video is ready."

• • •

Elle made sure her weapons were cleaned and her magazine was refilled. She sharpened her knife and checked her suit and burka. It didn't smell the best, but it was good enough for another night's work. Besides, she needed to look underprivileged since that was part of the plan. She was just finishing up when Eve walked in.

"Jack's ready for you. And, be ready, he's pretty proud of himself."

Elle couldn't help but smile as she followed Eve into the Ops center. Eve called it, Jack looked beyond pleased. If he could have puffed his chest out any further, he probably would have toppled over. She could see the video was up on all the screens, so she sat in her chair. "Ready when you are, maestro."

Jack gave a short preamble, "We had some great bones to work with on this clip but my software looped in our new dialogue perfectly, if I don't say so myself. Since they never really face the camera straight on, we had a lot of flexibility with the audio. But we made sure the jaw movement fit with the new sound."

He hit play with a little flourish, and Elle focused on the video on the screen. It was a brilliant piece of work. Jack kept as much of the original audio as possible, exchanging key words and phrases where necessary. If she hadn't heard the original first, she would have never picked up on the differences. The clip sounded like the target was completely sanguine about his ability to expose the Daesh leadership as corrupt, and that it was his moral obligation to see them removed from power. The other man's anxiety was played up, and his concerns about violence became assertions. It was seamless, and the only person who could refute the content would have a hard time convincing anyone once the target's death, under his roof, became public.

"I want this posted immediately with minimal flare. I want it to seem like 10 and 11 are in shock about the revelation, but that they received a preview of the evidence alluded to in the clip, and that convinced them to post the video. End the post with promises that the evidence would be posted later," Elle instructed.

"No problem. Acting like these two is easy now. No one seems to be the wiser," Jack said confidently.

"Be careful, Jack. Things are about to get intense fast. The possibility that our fake 10 and 11 could become targets in the coming days is extremely high. I wouldn't put it past the Daesh leadership to hire a black hat to track them, and we don't want any trace coming back to you. You'll need to be ready. You have to stay ahead of any attempts to find and target you."

Jack looked perplexed. It was obvious the thought had not occurred to him, but then he rallied. "I've got a few tricks up my sleeve. No one is going to track me."

"Don't get cocky, Jack. I know you're very good, but pride comes before the fall. These people have no conscience and unlimited resources. They could buy or coerce almost anyone they want if they felt pressed enough. You need to picture them finding an angle that would be your worst nightmare and stay out ahead of them."

Jack paled a little but nodded his understanding.

"Don't forget, Jack, get what you need done, cover your ass, and then sign off and get some sleep. Tomorrow, things are going to be crazy," She reminded.

"Yes, Mom." Jack replied.

Tex snorted, and Elle turned to see him covering a smile.

"You sending us to bed too, Mama?" he asked.

"If need be. You all have your marching orders. We get this right and by this time Friday, we'll be out of Iraq and heading to sunny Djibouti."

"Well now, there is some motivation. Do a good job, and you get to go to the armpit of civilization. Can't we go now? Please, please?" Tex asked.

Elle chuckled. "Alright, smart-ass, prep whatever you need to prep and get your sorry hide to bed. We're one step closer to mission complete."

Tex did an elaborate bow and walked out.

Eve walked over and said, "I've got Boy Wonder, I'll chase him out and send him to bed as soon as he's done. In the meantime, I'll prep for tomorrow. Do you need anything else?"

Elle shook her head and started to leave.

Eve stopped her and blurted, "I know you lost some faith in us, but we still believe in you. I'm sorry that things went the way they did the other day, but it was never meant to be a commentary on our interpersonal relationships. I consider you more than a leader or colleague. You're my friend, Elle. I'll always support you."

Elle was stunned. All she could do was incline her head to Eve and walk out.

Elle returned to her room and sat down on her bed. She was still thinking about what Eve said, and tried to identify what she was feeling. Moved by Eve's sentiment, and for reasons she wasn't ready to dwell on, she was touched. She took a few deep breaths and attempted to clear her mind. Focus was what she needed and, right now, sleep was critical; emotional turmoil was not just a nuisance but could be detrimental to her mission. Elle stretched out on her bed and put in her headphones. She chose Chopin's nocturnes and began meditating using the music as her point of focus. Eventually, she drifted off to sleep.

CHAPTER 13

When she woke, it felt like late afternoon. Elle grabbed her watch and confirmed her suspicions. She was irritated she'd slept so long. On the positive side, she was refreshed and didn't have any downtime to become distracted. She got up, went to the bathroom, and grabbed some food at the chow hall. The compound was active, but it was shift change. Everyone appeared to be minding their own business trying to get to or from work. She returned to her room and dressed in her suit before taking the food to the Ops center and sitting at her desk.

Jack, Eve, and Tex were all already working. They all looked up when she walked in and gave her various greetings before returning to their business. There was an energy in the room that said there would be a lot of updates coming her way. Eve was working on her mission brief, Tex was working on the logistics for their move, and Jack had several different programs running and the jihadist site up.

She started there. "What's the latest, Jack?"

"Oh, man, talk about kicking over a hornet's nest. It seems like everyone is losing their minds, and the site has almost crashed with the number of users checking out the video and leaving comments. There's a full-on battle going online right now. That video created a definite divide: those who are calling for the head of everyone involved in making the video, and those who are unnerved by it and asking questions about the referenced evidence. Those two groups have started turning on each other in the last hour. The private messages to the site are ugly. The profiles I've earmarked for the leadership are the worst. They're demanding the removal of the video with vivid threats about bodily harm and promises of swift retaliation for all involved," Jack reported.

"Perfect. I want you to take the worst private message threats and make them public. Feed the image that the leadership is corrupt and covering up after the major breech that Number 1 alluded to in our video. Say that you're being targeted because you were exposed to the truth," Elle said.

"You got it. I've also increased my security efforts. If anyone tries to trace me, I'll know about it. They'll have to go through multiple layers of protocol and traps before they even get close." Jack said and returned to his computers.

"Have they announced Number 1's death yet?" Elle asked.

"Not that we've found," Eve said. "I thought for sure we would have seen something by now. How can they keep something like that quiet?"

"I was counting on this. It's very dangerous ground for them. A senior member of Daesh that has a loyal following was killed under their roof. They were likely crafting their spin on it when our new video came out and destroyed their plans. I would imagine they're fielding or avoiding some very uncomfortable phone calls. They've never been forced into a position where they can't claim neutrality and take advantage of both sides. If they assume responsibility for the death, they'd be in good with the leadership. But, as you can see from the site, they'd be targeted by the growing opposition. They're desperately trying to craft a way out of their current predicament," Elle said.

"Not feeling any sympathy for them at all," Tex injected. "Those guys have been profiting off other people's suffering for years. They got it coming."

"Jack, once you get the threats posted on the site, I want you to pull some still images from the last bit of footage on the bedroom camera. They're gruesome, so prepare yourself. Wait until forty-five minutes before evening prayer tonight then post them. Claim the leadership was so afraid of what the target had on them, they had him murdered and cut out his tongue," Elle directed.

She braced for her team's judgement.

Jack turned a little green, Eve shifted uncomfortably, and Tex raised an eyebrow and pursed his lips; but to her surprise, they all recovered quickly and returned to what they were doing. She watched them for a few more moments before continuing, "Tex, we still on track for an 1830 departure?"

"Yep, just need you to confirm the infiltration and exfiltration coordinates so I can pass them to the pilots."

"I've got them here for you, Elle." Eve said. She put a map with the proposed coordinates up on the main monitor for her review.

Elle studied the terrain and the distances from her target location and decided they would work. She turned to Tex. "Go ahead and pass these. Let the pilots know their routes will need to swing wide of the city to avoid alerting the locals—no direct path in or out. I know the helo is as quiet as they get, but I want to mitigate any possible signature going in. I intend to fast-rope in at the infil point so there will be minimal time on target there. Eve, do you have a good landing zone where they can standoff and wait for my call for exfil?"

Eve walked over to the monitor and pointed to another area on the screen. "Terrain is good here for a landing zone, and it should be far enough away that the only chance of you running into anyone would be if a Bedouin happens to come along."

Both Tex and Elle looked at the location. "Looks like we have good line of sight there, too, so we would be able to see anyone coming at us from a distance. The only threat would be mortars. But, at night, the visibility would make it extremely difficult for anyone to try and set up on us and be successful," Tex said.

"I agree. That's what we'll go with. Let the pilots know," Elle ordered, and she went and settled down behind her desk to eat and prepare for her next task.

Over the next couple of hours, Elle watched the news and prepped her equipment for the mission. Everything was functioning just how she wanted it, and the team was working together like the stellar group it was. These moments were prime and the reason her team was as successful as it was. They had surprised her with their acceptance and loyalty. Looking at them, she realized that she wasn't the only one who had been forced to adjust to recent events.

Just before 1800, Elle went to her room and the prep area to retrieve her things. There was no need to bother with the burka for now since she wouldn't need it until she was within the city limits of Al Qaim. She armed herself with her knife and both her SIGs this time—one in the ankle holster and the other in the small of her back. She kept her pack light and only included her night vision goggles (NVGs), a GPS, headlamp, small tool kit, gloves, a protein bar, and some water. She didn't anticipate needing any of the items, but she always factored in the potential for her plans to go to shit unexpectedly. She'd never be able to counter everything that could go wrong, but she could try to mitigate for some of the worst-case scenarios.

She returned to the Ops center, and Tex was there in tactical gear, looking ready for action. Eve was putting the brief up on the monitor and Jack was typing away. She went to him first and looked over his shoulder. He was putting together the post with the pictures of Number 1's corpse, just as she'd requested.

Jack jumped when he realized she was standing next to him. "This is going to send shockwaves through…well…everything."

"That's the point. It's pretty hard for an enemy to remain effective on the battlefield, and on the world stage, when it's fighting itself. This is just the beginning. That bloodlust and fanaticism that the Daesh leadership cultivates is about to bite the hand that feeds it."

"I pulled a couple of pretty vivid screen shots, and I've been debating on the verbiage for the accompanying post. Any thoughts?" Jack asked.

Elle read over his shoulder. "Go with the second option, scared but defiant. And add a touch of righteous fervor."

Jack added some ideological crap that was likely a favorite post of either 10 or 11.

Elle read as he typed.

"That should do it," he said. "Eve what time is evening prayer tonight?"

"It's at 2029 here in Baghdad, and it will be 2048 in Al Qaim."

Prayer times are calculated based on the movement of the sun, so evening prayer could be at very different times depending on how far east or west you were. Since Elle would be leaving central Iraq for as far west in the country as she could go, the prayer times were just shy of twenty minutes apart. Since timing was a factor in her plans, those details were the kind of things that could make or break her mission.

"Post that at 2015. Enough time for people here in Baghdad to start talking about it and carry the chatter into the mosques. That chatter will flow out quickly from the capital and should reach even the people in the western provinces by the time they go to prayer. The major players will be pulling out all the stops to get as much information as possible and to assess how it will impact them. They'll run to their power bases, and they'll make mistakes that we're going to exploit." Elle moved to her desk and sat down. "Eve, are you ready to brief?"

Eve nodded, moved to the screen, and began her brief, "I've been pouring through every resource I could think of and no one is talking about any deaths within the Daesh ranks. There are discussions about a disturbance in the Karada District, but the assessments are all speculation based on rumors that there was a break-in. Most are assuming that something of value was stolen and that it's being kept quiet because it was illegal. The favorite theory is stolen museum pieces with a few going with weapons. There are several reports of sectarian violence within Baghdad and a report of an IED emplacement on the main route into Nasser Wa Salaam. That was likely some attempt at retaliation for the SOF mission that happened there last night. One report of note is the increase in the activity at the Syrian border by Al Qaim. Analysts are suggesting that Daesh is funneling forces and support through that part of the border and building a western front to fortify what it already controls and to flank opposition forces." Eve paused for questions or comments.

Elle nodded for her to continue. This development would bode well for her plans tonight if accurate.

"Tonight, is going to be cloudy, so illumination will be sparse. And, wind will be picking up from the west after midnight due to a series of storms moving in that are expected to hit in the early morning hours tomorrow and move east over the next couple of days. We were able to pull overhead imagery and, after some traffic pattern analysis, we're confident that we have the correct location for Number 8's hawala. Prime operational times are late morning and early evening. No new information about a bed down location."

Elle smiled. "If things play out like I think they will, that will not be an issue. All those Daesh members traveling through the area will need to receive funds. They aren't likely to do a lot of business in daylight hours. It would just make them easier to track. Add in the havoc we're about to cause with the revelation of Number 1's death, and the likelihood that 8 will be heading into work tonight is exponentially higher. I'll be heading to the hawala. Can you bring up an overhead and show me the most likely route from the mosques to the hawala?

Eve walked over to her computer, pulled up an overhead image, and dropped points to show the locations that Elle requested. "It looks like all the roads funnel down and there are two probable routes to the hawala, here and here." Eve highlighted them.

Elle studied the image. She took in terrain features, the surrounding infrastructure, and zoned in on the corner directly behind the hawala. Her gut was saying that 8 would use the back entrance to return to his place of business which would allow him some time before opening the main entrance for his "customers." He would want to get a head start and be sure he was prepared for anything that could happen. And after the revelation Jack was about to make on their jihadist forums, 8 would be keen to try and prepare for an onslaught of agitated terrorists.

Elle was ready. She looked at her team and smiled. "Excellent work as always. Jack, watch your timeline. Eve, help him out. You ready to head out, Tex?"

Tex acted like he was considering, and then said, "I suppose I am."

"Oh, thank you so much for penciling me into your schedule. Would you care to escort me to the party?"

He stood up primly, gave a regal half-bow, and extended his arm.

Elle took it. As they started walking, she twisted her inside leg up and landed a swift kick on his backside.

Eve and Jack burst out laughing.

Tex stutter-stepped.

Elle just kept a straight face as though nothing had happened and kept walking.

The sun was low in the sky when they left their building and got into the car. It wasn't a long distance to the helo pad, but they wanted to avoid drawing curious stares as much as possible. They rode in silence for the few minutes it took to get to the location.

When they parked, she turned to him. "After you brief everyone and they're ready to go, signal me, and I'll come up then. Once we are in the air, I'll avoid the main channel on the headphones, so give me an alternate that will just be for the two of us. When they grasp that I'm not going to engage with them, they should lose interest in me and focus on the mission."

"Not sure why you're so concerned. It's not like anything about this mission or you doing it is unusual," he replied. Then he grinned, got out, and jogged to the helo.

Elle watched as he approached the bird, and that's when the men standing by it turned around, and her heart stopped. She cursed under her breath as she saw that both Julian and Red Shirt were there. They were kitted up and carrying sniper rifles. They were the shooters that Tex had acquired for her mission. She could feel her heart racing, the blood surged through her veins, and her stomach turned a little. Fucking Murphy's Law bit her in the ass hard this time.

She realized she was holding her breath and exhaled. While this was not ideal, she could handle it. Besides, they would be leaving after the completion of this mission, so any complications that developed because of this—unexpected turn of events, she wouldn't have to deal with long. They would all be out of sight, out of mind soon enough. Elle needed to keep herself on track, she had a job to do, and these two were not her main problem.

Forcing her mind back to the task at hand, she ran through her mental checklists. She continued to breathe deeply to bring her body back under her control and put her emotions back in check. She needed to remain detached and focused, and the men were not factors in her overall goal. If they could do their job, she didn't care what they thought about her or what was happening. Given their positions, and probable expertise, she was confident that neither would allow a failure on their watch. Her pulse settled back into rhythm and her head cleared. She only saw the tasks in front of her.

The pilot went to the cockpit while the copilot stood by on the ground. She could see them going through their startup procedures. It was almost time. Elle grabbed her bag and double checked her gear and weapons. She looked up when she saw motion out of the corner of her eye. The shooters were boarding, and Tex was waiting for them to get set before he signaled her. She cracked the door of the car and waited. As the blades started to turn, the copilot watched for any issues as they got up to speed. Once he was satisfied that the bird was full mission capable, he boarded. Tex signaled for her.

Elle got out of the car and jogged to the helicopter. She caught Tex's outstretched hand and jumped onboard in one fluid motion. She felt eyes on her and looked up to see Red Shirt looking like he thought this must be some kind of joke. It was easy to read his lips: *You've got to be fucking kidding me.*

Julian raised an eyebrow and gave her a half smile. She could see interest in his eyes when he looked at her, but all he did was incline his head to her and then return to the business at hand. She did not acknowledge either of the shooters, as Tex handed her a headset. He held up one finger and then three, letting her know that the crew was on Channel One but that the two of them would be on Channel Three. She nodded and moved to the back of the bird, as far from the shooters as possible. Tex sat in the jump seat next to her, and they waited for take-off.

Elle turned to Channel One to listen to the crew. The pilots were going through standard take-off procedures. When they checked to make sure the crew was ready to go, Red Shirt tried to get a rise out of her by answering in an effeminate voice, "It's just us girls back here, so make sure you take it easy on us. We're delicate."

Elle felt him staring at her, waiting for a reaction, but she refused to give him the satisfaction. Eventually, he answered that he was ready and that the portside was clear for take-off.

Julian answered with a simple, "Set, clear on the starboard side."

She sat back and closed her eyes, allowing Tex to roger up for them. Once that was done, she could feel the bird lift off.

After they were airborne, the pilot said it was about two hours until they reached their destination. He reminded his passengers that, while the helicopter had stealth technology, it was not silent or invisible. All aircraft signatures were greatly reduced, but light discipline was critical. Since the drop zone was only three miles outside the city, the inhabitants would hear the noise. It would sound different from the aircraft they were used to hearing, though, so the less time spent hovering, the better.

She glanced at Tex and shrugged her shoulders nonchalantly. Tex spoke up for her and assured them that would not be an issue, and he added that the time at the drop zone would be minimal. She felt her skin crawl and knew Red Shirt was watching her. She used her peripheral vision to confirm her suspicions. The jackass was smirking and looked like a giant baboon. He obviously thought this was some kind of ploy, and appeared like he was waiting to mock her when she made a mistake, or the rouse was exposed.

Elle chanced a glance over at Julian, and he was focused on his job, scanning the ground, watching for any potential threat. It didn't seem as though he cared about her presence at all. He was brought in for a job and he was going to see it executed flawlessly. She respected his professionalism and focus. At least one of the shooters was proving to be exactly what she was looking for. She had to assume, like all sociopaths, Red Shirt was excellent at selling his greatness to others. The jerk likely had talent, but it was probably overinflated to feed his narcissism.

She nudged Tex. When he looked over, she moved her hand to change the channel on the headset. He followed her lead.

"You do realize that's the sociopath that I pulled Eve away from?"

Tex nodded. "I suspected he was. He fit Eve's description, and has been acting like a world-class jackass ever since he saw me, but I couldn't exactly swap him out then. All I had was his name and the recommendation from the team that he was one of their best. He's a piece of work, but if he gets twitchy, I'll just toss his ass out of the bird."

"It won't be direct, so be on guard. You need to trust me on this. He's a problem. Don't give him any advantage. I'll be gone for about two hours depending on how long it takes for the target to show. I'll signal you on the satellite phone when I'm en route to the extraction point."

"Copy all. How long should we wait before we come in after you?"

Elle paused before she answered, "You don't."

Tex stared at her like he was waiting for a punchline. "You can't be serious," he said.

"If I fail, the mission is over. Period. You guys return to base, you pack up the office, and you take the team home to debrief and await reassignment."

"That's complete horseshit, Elle, and it doesn't have to—"

Elle cut Tex off with a hand signal, then shifted her eyes to Red Shirt. Tex understood her; their conversation was no longer private.

He wanted to re-engage. Elle refused to acknowledge him. She turned back to the main radio channel, leaned back in her seat; and closed her eyes again. He had her orders; they weren't open for debate. They all needed to focus on the mission at hand. She cleared her head and allowed the rhythm and motion of the helo to relax her.

Over the next two hours, Red Shirt tried to engage Tex in some occasional banter, probably trying to build rapport. Otherwise, the radio channel stayed clear. Elle allowed herself to doze off, making the best use of the time by resting. She didn't anticipate being out too long tonight, but she had to cover a lot of ground during this mission, and there was always the possibility things could go awry. Conserving energy and resting while she was able was a smart move.

There were none of the usual telltale signs, but she knew on some level that someone was watching her. When she opened her eyes, she looked right into Julian's and felt her body warm. He didn't look away or seem bothered at all that she'd caught him looking.

Elle glanced at her watch and saw that it was almost time. The pilots confirmed her estimate when they announced over the radio that the bird was ten minutes away from the drop zone.

Tex looked over at her and nodded and then made sure the rope was set up correctly for her descent. She checked her gear, making certain everything was properly stowed for her to fast rope out of the helo the second they arrived at the infil point. She pulled on her gloves and checked her shoes. The instep had a special coating to help it resist melting from the friction of the rope, and she ensured her laces and pant legs were secured.

Elle squared her shoulders and joined Tex at the port side of the aircraft. Red Shirt made room for them with a mocking sweeping bow. He obviously thought this was all some kind of stunt. She removed her headset and handed it to Tex. She would rely entirely on his direction from this point on. That's all she would need. She scanned the exterior of the helo as she waited for the rope to be set up. She was ready. Movement caught her eye and she turned her head to see Julian repositioning himself to have a better angle to cover her. He smiled and winked before he returned his attention to his job. Elle took her headscarf and fastened it around her face to protect against the sand and dust kicked up by the wash of the blades. Then, she pulled on her night-vision goggles.

Tex signaled that they were one minute out; he moved into position, and Elle braced herself using an overhead handhold. She kept her focus on him, he knew exactly what he was doing, and she was counting on him to keep this crew in line while she was gone. He wouldn't let her down. Tex held up one fist letting her know the final countdown was coming, then his fingers counted down from five. When he hit zero, he pushed the door open and kicked out the rope. She didn't hesitate.

Elle grabbed it and hopped out of the bird, swinging her body around in one fluid movement until she was facing the helicopter. She kept one hand on top of the other and her elbows out to control her speed of descent, while simultaneously capturing the rope between the instep and bottom of her feet. She moved quickly down the rope. Just before reaching the ground, she let go of the rope with her feet and cushioned her touch down by bending her knees to absorb the shock and keep her balance. She was on the ground in a few seconds and started to jog to town.

The helo was quieter, and operated at a different octave, so it was easy to see how it did not raise alarms on the ground like a normal helicopter would. But, it still kicked up a hell of a mess.

Elle kept running as quickly as she could in the darkness, careful to keep an eye on her footing. Eve had been right; illumination was almost nonexistent to the naked eye. But breaks in the clouds and the city in the distance, provided enough ambient light for the night-vision goggles. It was always an adjustment when wearing the NVGs because it skewed depth perception for the first couple of feet. She'd done it enough that she automatically compensated and was mentally mapping the terrain to avoid letting her eyes be deceived by what they perceived as being directly in front of her. She heard the helo pull up and bank away, but she didn't turn around. They had their orders, and she had a job to do and three miles to cover to get to it.

Elle fell into a steady rhythm as she ran. She kept her breathing under control, and her mind focused. One wrong step and this mission was over. It was a cool, overcast night, and the quiet was almost complete. Every so often, she saw movement on her flanks and knew it was likely wild dogs or jackals. Their prey drive was triggered by her movement, but her smell and size were keeping them at a distance. She hoped none of them were desperate or sick enough to make a try for her. She didn't want to waste a bullet or risk alerting the two-legged animals she knew were close.

Other than the dogs, the area was clear. She could smell dirt and burning trash but, as far as Iraq went, the night air was almost refreshing. Elle needed to cover the miles as quickly as possible and get into position. As soon as evening prayer was over, her target would be on the move, and she needed to be ready.

Elle began to make out the silhouette of buildings and slowed her speed so she could scan for activity. The buildings appeared to be homes, and, given the lack of movement, the occupants were either away or in a room without windows. She moved into the deeper shadows around one of the homes, removed her NVGs, and put on her burka and headscarf. Her eyes adjusted to the low light coming from a handful of street lamps. She took a moment to check her GPS to confirm her location, and left the shadows.

It was the biggest risk she was taking tonight. Walking through Al Qaim alone was welcoming trouble. Any man seeing her out alone could take offense and bring a lot of problems her way. She made an effort to walk in the deepest shadows along her route and constantly scanned her surroundings; she needed to be her own early warning system. The buildings were old and rundown but well maintained. The sidewalks were broken, and the trash was pushed into piles between the buildings. Once she got into areas that were more heavily occupied by businesses, the shadows were harder to come by. Gaudy neon lights labeled various businesses while dingy street lights attempted to be more inviting than ominous.

Elle kept her head down. She could see movement inside the various shops, likely those left behind to watch the businesses while the owners went to prayer at the mosques. She wasn't far from her target location, and the sooner she got there, the better. A loud crash made her stop short and whip her head around. A jackal went flying past her, scared away by the metal can it knocked over. She moved over to the next alley and ducked into it to avoid being spotted by anyone disturbed by the racket. She paused for a few moments and, when she didn't hear anything, chanced a look around. It was clear, so she used the alley as a cut-through and returned to her route.

As she rounded the next corner, she could see her target area in the distance. She shifted her walk to a limp and rounded her shoulders. Anyone looking at her would assume she was an old, broken woman and become disinterested, buying her time. She had moved her bag to her front, so it appeared she had a large belly in case anyone paid her a second glance. Elle's intent was to mask her appearance as much as possible while simultaneously making herself seem weak and inconsequential. She needed to be invisible, but when she wasn't, completely underestimated.

She made it to her target area without anyone seeming to pay her any mind. As she approached the building that Eve had postulated as being the hawala, she saw several men in the shadows across the street from what would be the front door. The hair on the back of her neck stood on end and she angled away from their line of sight. Number 8 had anxious customers waiting outside already; Elle was sure of it. She passed the rear entrance to the shop and a man walked out of the shadows toward her. He sneered and shifted his weight as if he were sizing her up. This was what she had hoped to avoid, a bully looking to find some entertainment.

The man strode over and asked her what she was doing out alone; Elle just stood still and swayed slightly back and forth muttering slightly under her breath. The man crowded her and demanded an answer. Elle started with a ragged cough, held out a shaking hand and said in Arabic "money, please." The man pulled back disgusted, and told her to go home. She kept up the act, adding that her husband said to get money. The man finally backed away and left to link up with the men at the front of the building. They would all likely leave her alone now. Sadly, it wasn't unusual for men to force their wives to beg for money, and she was counting on the disdain of others.

She hobbled her way over to the intersection that was behind the hawala and sat down. She held her hand out like a beggar and swayed slightly every so often. She could hear the men in front of the hawala having loud discussions. It was difficult to pick up what was said from that distance, but she was fairly certain they were arguing over the revelation of the Imam's death and the allegations made on the websites. Elle smiled. Things were playing out exactly as she thought they would. Now, all she needed was her target. She looked around and reassessed what she saw from the satellite photos. It was still the best position for her to wait for Number 8 to return to his shop, and she was confident that he would. The chaos caused by their latest fabricated post would make it inevitable.

Time passed slowly, but it wasn't long before she heard footsteps echoing off the pavement to her left. Using her peripheral vision, she watched the approach of a man. She judged his build to be in line with her target, but the shadows obscured his face. She continued with her ruse and scanned the area to see if anyone was within view. Things could get complicated if he made too much of a ruckus, but she had already planned several escape routes pending the results of the next few minutes. She held her knife along the inside of her arm and waited for a positive ID.

Number 8 stepped into the light of one of the old street lamps, and she got it. She also noticed that he seemed irritated at her sitting so close to his business begging for money. It must happen frequently, from the look on his face. He walked directly toward her and started trying to shoo her away, insisting he would call his security and have her removed by force. Her muscles tensed, ready to strike. Things were about to go crazy around here.

Elle waited until Number 8 was right on top of her. He turned toward his shop to yell for security, and she shot her blade across the back of his ankle cutting his Achilles tendon. The shock of the attack robbed him of his voice, and his body went crashing to the ground as his body reacted to the pain. She was on him instantly covering his mouth and slitting his throat. She jumped to her feet and pulled 8 into the shadows. He was still struggling, but the only sound he could make was a reedy gurgling and tiny squeal.

His body convulsed making it harder to move him, but she needed to buy herself some time. She couldn't risk one of the men waiting for 8's return to spot him lying on the ground. The security personnel were likely to come looking for him shortly after his arrival time passed. Moving the body would keep them from seeing something was wrong until they arrived at the blood stains on the ground.

It wasn't perfect, and the man was still in the throes of death, but she had to go. 8 was a dead man. The severed Achilles meant he couldn't do anything more than crawl, and he couldn't call out because of the slit to his throat. He would be dead in moments. Even if help were to arrive in the next couple of minutes, it would be too late. The only question was: how much time did she have before she had pursuit?

She returned to her ruse of the hunched, hobbled woman and made her way back via the route she'd come. She needed to maintain the illusion for as long as possible, but felt time running out. She turned the corner just as she heard a shout of alarm. She couldn't tell what was said, but knew they had found 8's body. It was time to move. She ran, uncaring what attention it brought, no way of avoiding scrutiny at this point. A woman had been seen at the site where the body was found. Even if they didn't want to believe that a woman was capable of the crime, it would take them seconds to piece together that she was a suspect at the very least.

There were far too many people out, and they were all watching the strange scene of a woman running wildly down the road for no apparent reason. She needed to get out of the business areas, and into less travelled neighborhoods. It was a gamble but one she needed to take. Relying on the map in her head, she veered onto a darker road and pulled out the satellite phone as she sprinted. She dialed Tex, and, when he answered, she wasted no time. "Need immediate extract, ETA twenty-four minutes, high probability of hostile presence."

"Copy all, moving. Coming in hot."

Elle slowed long enough to return the phone to her pack, remove her costume, and put her NVGs and scarf back in place. She swung the bag onto her back, retrieved her pistol, and, holding on to her knife for luck, took off at a dead run. Moving a lot faster than normal, she stumbled a couple of times, but gained her equilibrium after a few adjustments to her mental calculations.

Elle sensed her pursuers and dove for cover. Seconds later, a pickup truck came into view. Elle pulled back to make certain the headlights didn't burn her eyes through the NVGs. They had searchlights and were searching both the roads and the buildings, looking for any clue as to where she went. Elle still had an advantage. They assumed she was Iraqi, and that she was hiding somewhere in the village. Not willing to risk that an occupant of the vehicle had their own NVGs, she waited until the truck rolled over to the next block. The wait cost her several minutes that she needed to make up. She took one last breath and bolted. It was only a matter of time before they searched outside the town.

Elle ran as fast as she dared given the NVGs and terrain. Her heart was pounding in her chest and her breathing was getting heavy. She was in shape, but this was a challenge. She needed to keep pushing hard, so she focused on her body, willing her heart rate to slow which eased her breathing a little. It was meditation and focus applied to the physical world. The effect was marginal, but she would take anything she could get. She estimated that she was halfway to her extraction point, in another twelve to fifteen minutes she would be out of there.

She heard the low frequency she knew was the helo; and was so intent on it that she almost missed the high-pitched whistle of the bullet flying past her. *Shit, here we go.* She didn't turn to look. Elle noticed the ground in front of her lighten, the vehicle's headlights were starting to illuminate her. She sprinted forward, weaving erratically to make hitting her difficult. There was no way she was going to outrun them, so she made as much forward progress as possible and then dove behind some broken rocks.

The truck hadn't anticipated her move, so it ended up skidding to a halt just past her position. She vaulted over the rocks, putting them between her and the truck just as the spotlight lit up the area. She froze and waited. Elle heard the helo getting closer, and knew that they had to be able to see the headlights of the truck and would be coming for her. She couldn't let these men live to talk about what they saw here, but it was going to be tricky. If they made a run for it, they could get back to town before the snipers in the helo could take them out. She made her decision.

They were still searching for her with the light when she sprinted out from behind the rock and jumped into the bed of the truck. She used the glass breaker on the end of her knife to smash out the window and started shooting. Elle went for the driver first; and was able to take out two of the four men in the truck before the passenger began to return fire. Elle threw herself over the side, and rolled under the bed.

She heard arguing and then the doors opened and both remaining men got out to pursue her. Once they were out of the truck, she shot them both in the ankles, and, when they dropped to the ground, she shot one in the head and the other in the chest. Crawling out from under the truck, she ran for the landing helo. She was steps away from the bird when a burning pain shot through her right shoulder and she pitched forward. Somehow, she managed to keep on her feet. She leaped and caught Tex's outstretched hand just as Red Shirt fired at a target behind her. The passenger of the truck must have still had some life in him because he managed to get a shot off.

The smug expression on Red Shirt's face told her that at least the man was dead now.

CHAPTER 14

She returned to her seat and put pressure on her wound as the bird took off. Tex was by her side in seconds with a medical kit and shoved headphones on her, allowing no refusal. "Talk to me, Elle, and none of your usual shit."

"It's a through and through, doesn't feel like anything is broken. But it hurts like a mother fucker and it's bleeding like crazy."

He grabbed her arm, and cut the fabric to get at the source of the bleeding. Once he assessed the damage, he packed the wound with an impossible amount of gauze and used a pressure bandage to hold it all in place. It felt like he was ripping her arm wide open, and the pressure was almost unbearable, but she knew it needed to be done. If they didn't get the bleeding under control immediately, she was in a world of trouble. Her body broke out in a sweat from the pain, and she felt nauseous, but she endured his ministrations stoically.

She tried to distract herself from the pain by looking around the helo; that was a mistake. Red Shirt was practically preening. Elle could see him relishing the story he was building in his head. He would be expecting her to be falling all over him in gratitude. She couldn't wait to disappoint him. She would thank him out of professional courtesy, but if he had been half a good as he thought he was, that asshole wouldn't have gotten off a shot at all.

Elle looked over to Julian and he was, once again, the model of professionalism, on full alert watching for additional hostile forces. She watched him for a while, which, he must have sensed because he looked over and met her eyes. He looked concerned and cocked his head slightly as if asking her if everything was okay. She nodded. He inclined his head and returned to scanning for threats. Strange, not a single word passed between them, but it was like they understood each other perfectly. That comforted her for some reason.

She snapped back to Tex when he tested her arm for breaks, and she almost punched him. "Easy, asshole. I told you I didn't think anything was broken, but that doesn't give you permission to go crazy."

"Deal with it, Elle. I know you've had worse, so stop bellyaching. This is going to need medical attention when we get back. That could push your timetable to the right."

"No, stay with the plan. A few stitches and some antibiotics, and I'll be fine. We can't afford to stick around any longer. Red Shirt is practically salivating over his hero fantasies, and we don't want his brand of crazy around us any longer. Tonight's little adventure is going to draw too much attention. We need to leave, and let things settle back to normal. Then we'll just be another war story that gets told over a few beers."

"Damn, you're cynical," Tex said.

"Hell, I thought I was being optimistic," Elle replied with a wane smile.

"I suppose for you it was. Buckle in and try to get some rest. Between the blood loss and you trying to keep your crazy schedule when we land, you're going to need to take what you can. I'll handle the crew, and have a medic standing by when we hit the deck."

Tex squeezed her other shoulder and held her gaze for a moment longer giving her a slight nod, a sign of solidarity and letting her know that he was glad she made it back. She returned his nod and leaned back in her seat. She was tired and sore. Sleep would be necessary for her to have any hope of making it through these next twenty-four hours. So, she did her best to block out the pain and shut off her brain for a little while. She focused in on the low vibrations and the rhythm of the helo again, and slept.

Elle woke with a start, in what seemed like only moments later, but quickly realized she had slept the entire flight. Tex, who had nudged her awake, was pointing to the headset and indicated Channel One. Elle flipped the channel and heard the pilots discussing landing preparations. They were five minutes out. She started to check her gear when a jolt of white-hot pain reminded her that she wasn't at 100 percent. She grimaced and moved a little slower, testing her range and capability. She could use the arm, but under heavy protest, and she doubted that she would have much strength or flexibility for a little while. *Shit.* This was going to complicate her plans.

Managing to get her gear in order and set before landing, Elle glanced around and saw Red Shirt still smirking, and Julian leaned back in his seat with his eyes closed. They really needed to be out of this bird and on their way out of town. A pang of guilt went through her at the thought of the questions Tex would have to dodge during the mission debrief, but that was part of his job description; wrangler. At least he enjoyed handling the knuckle draggers. He liked being in their world, and it made him feel like he always had a leg up on them.

Her momentary guilt disappeared—and then she looked out the side of the helo and saw a figure waiting for them. Eve. Damnit, Tex had called Eve in to get her to the medic. Rationally, Elle knew that it was the best move, but she could imagine the worried look on the woman's face already, and she didn't want that. Eve was the best option, though. If anyone started asking too many questions, Eve could easily play the worried friend and get them back on task to ease her distress.

When they touched down, Elle waited for the pilot to give the all clear to disembark. Red Shirt was waiting for her with an expectant look. She inclined her head and kept moving. He grabbed her arm. She wanted to punch him, but her shoulder wound prevented it. Instead, she turned and faced him directly.

He was seething. "You need to learn some respect."

"Funny, I was just thinking the same thing."

His fingers bit hard into her arm. Elle felt like he wanted to strike her but then suddenly realized they weren't alone. Red Shirt looked up and saw Tex and Julian moving their way. He gave her one last venomous look, let her go, and stepped back.

"You owe me, bitch. I'll be collecting soon."

"Looking forward to it."

Eve met Elle halfway and started to throw her arms around her but restrained herself. Worry was coming off Eve in waves. They walked back to the car, and Elle got in to find water and a blanket waiting. She took a long drink. Eve jumped into the driver's seat and put the car in gear.

"Seriously, Elle, are you okay? Do you need anything?"

"I'm going to be just fine. Believe me, I've had worse." She leaned back into the seat and tried to relax as Eve drove around the compound toward the medical facility. Another benefit to being in the same location as the special forces guys is that they had their own medical facility. Given the nature of their work, it was top notch, and they understood sensitive operations. She wasn't looking forward to this, though. She hated hospitals and needles. She would much rather get shot again, but that wouldn't help her get to the next part of her mission any faster.

Elle tried to relax and changed the topic. "How's everything going in the office? Has Jack run into any issues?"

"The jihadist forums have gone nuclear after that post to the website. It spread like wildfire, and it looks like a full-fledged civil war is breaking out in Daesh. They're turning on each other left and right. Two main factions are gaining traction, but there are numerous splinter elements that have differing perspectives. I imagine those will be pulled into one of the main elements soon enough, but the divide in the major split is clear: loyalty to the leadership or overthrow the corrupt traitors to the cause. Jack has been having a hard time keeping tabs on all the activity. He says that there have been two attempts to trace him since the post, and he thinks he'll only be able to hold them off for a little longer."

"He won't have to. I think it's time for him to put his borrowed personas into hiding. Have him post that they fear for their lives and suspect that the leadership is trying to have them killed. He needs to claim that they already survived one attempt, so they're going into hiding to make sure that someone who knows the truth will survive."

"I'll tell him, but first I need to get you taken care of."

"I'll be fine, just drop me off and then you can get back to Jack. Time is a factor with this."

Eve pursed her lips. Elle could see she was fighting back a retort.

After a moment, she regained her composure and replied, "I'll give Jack his instructions, but not until you're taken care of, Elle." She held up a hand to stop Elle's protest. "Save your breath. You can order me around all you want, but I'm going to ignore anything that doesn't have me staying with you until you get attended to by a medical professional. Fire me if you want, but I'm still doing it."

"Fine. You can wait. But that'll mean Jack and Tex will need to continue packing without you. I'm sure there are better ways to avoid packing the office than waiting around in a hospital. I'll be just fine."

"The boys can handle things without me, and, despite your feelings about it, it would be better for someone else to be there to keep anyone from getting too interested in you."

Elle couldn't help but chuckle; Eve had used her own thought process against her and won. Eve was right, she could easily play the distressed friend and keep the focus on her and deflect all questions about Elle with concerns for better comfort and care. "If I didn't know better, Eve, I'd say you just manipulated me."

"Would I do that?" Eve asked. "That would imply that I actually pay attention to all the crap you throw out."

This time Elle laughed outright, grimacing a little from the pain it caused. "Crap, huh? Noted."

They reached the medical unit, and Elle got out of the car.

Eve ran around to catch up with her. They walked into the facility.

Eve walked to the reception area and introduced herself. "I called about the gunshot wound to the shoulder. The doctor is waiting for us."

The kid behind the counter looked at Elle wide eyed, and his gaze dropped to the bandage on her shoulder. He jumped to his feet. "Yes ma'am, this way please."

They followed the kid into a room, and he closed the door. "Ma'am, I need to get some vitals from you for the doctor." He gestured to the exam table and a hospital gown. "Please change out of your clothes, and put on the gown if possible. If you need help, we can have one of the nurses come in to assist."

Elle shook her head. "I'm good. Just need a few minutes."

The kid nodded and left the room.

Elle removed her gear and handed it to Eve. "Please don't let anyone mess with this." Her shirt was trashed, but it was still intact so this part was going to be fun. She went into her pack and retrieved her knife. It was still covered in blood since she didn't clean it before she had to run. Elle took the blade to the sink and cleaned it off and dried it before she used the mirror to help her cut the arm off her shirt.

Eve's face lost color when she saw the blade, but snapped out of her shock when she realized what Elle was doing. "Give me that," she demanded.

Elle hesitated for a moment, then handed her the knife, handle first. Eve was overly cautious at first, being unfamiliar with the blade's sharpness, but she quickly figured it out and made short work of Elle's sleeve. Once the material was off the arm, it was fairly simple to remove the rest of the shirt.

Elle got into the hospital gown while Eve folded her clothing, setting them aside. "You could probably make the shirt sleeveless if you want to keep it," she said randomly.

"I suppose it would be a waste to lose it just because of a missing sleeve."

She had just sat on the exam table when there was a tentative knock on the door. The kid had returned and began taking her blood pressure and temperature. He asked about her height, weight, current medications, and medical history. Then, he asked about her pain and the circumstances of her wound. She answered the pain scale question with a seven out of ten and then left the circumstances of her injury as a "philosophical dispute." The kid looked like he was going to press the issue for a moment, but then rethought things when he saw the ice-cold look on Elle's face. He wisely did not ask any more questions and excused himself to go and prep for X-rays.

When he left, Eve asked, "What do you think they are going to do with you?"

Elle started to shrug and stopped herself. "Best case, I get some stitches. Worst case, I need surgery to repair anything torn up inside."

"You don't seem concerned."

"I'm not. At this point it's more of a hindrance and irritation. But I have no choice. I have to get this taken care of before I can press forward."

"That's a very clinical way of looking at it."

"How else would I look at it?" Elle asked rhetorically. "I'm not going to start acting any different, find religion, or change my wicked ways. This is always a very real possibility every time I take a job. I accepted that a long time ago, and it doesn't bother me. The task was completed, I'm alive, and the guy who shot me isn't. I would call that a success."

Eve started to reply when the knock on the door signaled the medic's return. He led Elle to the X-ray room, and they took film from several angles. When she returned, Eve was waiting. "You know you can go anytime. It's going to be pretty standard now depending on what the doctor sees on the X-ray." Elle said.

"I'll be sticking around until we know what the deal is at the very least. Longer if needed—or wanted." Elle sighed. She didn't feel like arguing with her.

When she returned to the table, she noticed her iPod sitting out. She raised an eyebrow at Eve.

"I figured there would be some waiting involved in all of this and that you might want your music."

Elle was surprised by Eve's correct assumptions. "Does that mean that you're leaving after all?"

"No, I'm still staying, but I don't want to make this worse for you."

Elle felt her chest tighten, and she blinked rapidly a couple of times because her eyes burned a little. The woman really was a saint, and Elle couldn't deny that she felt affection for her. All she could manage at that moment was a quiet thank you.

They sat in a comfortable silence until the next knock on the door sounded and the doctor came in. He introduced himself and began to go over his findings. They weren't what she hoped, but they weren't the worst either. The bullet tore through muscle tissue, ligaments, and nicked the bone. There were bone fragments in the wound that needed to be removed to keep them from causing future complications or potentially puncturing veins and arteries.

The staff was prepping for the surgery now, and she began the process of signing forms and going through the tedium of being warned about the risks associated with anesthetics. She tried to get them to do a local but the doctor refused. He was not willing to risk her moving during surgery and causing further damage, and ignored her assertions that it would not be an issue. He anticipated the surgery taking two hours with a few hours in recovery. She would stay in observation for at least twenty-four hours. Elle started to protest but Eve interrupted her and told the doctor they understood.

Elle glared at her when the doctor left. "What the hell was that?"

"Easy, Elle. Arguing with the man about to cut you isn't a very smart prospect. Neither is putting additional time constraints on him. You can't force your will on everyone and expect it to pan out well. You need to let this play out. Focus on the first hurdle in front of you, which is the surgery, then the recovery, then getting back to work. We can adjust as needed, and the guys and I can keep the mission going as planned until you can link back up. You need to put your ego in check and be smart about this."

Once again, Elle was stunned. She wasn't sure if what she was feeling was pride or discontent, or both. Regardless, Eve was right. As much as she hated to admit it, and to acknowledge that her plan would have to change, she needed to suck it up and adjust. Elle sat down and took a few deep breaths to regain her composure and conceded, "You're right. But that means that you'll need to be in the office and not here."

"I already said I would go when we knew the deal, Elle. As soon as they take you into surgery, I'll go back. One of us will be here to check on you every hour until you're allowed visitors. At that point, we'll bring you up to speed on our progress and you can come up with a new plan based on that and what your doctor tells you."

"Yes, Mom." Elle said.

"Behave yourself, young lady, and you might get some ice cream."

Elle laughed. "Deal. Now go ahead and get out of here. I'm going to listen to my music until they come and get me."

"Go ahead and listen to whatever you want, Elle, but I'm not going until they take you in for surgery. I'm here for moral support." Eve sat back in the chair and grabbed an old magazine off a desk and flipped it open.

Elle put in her headphones and laid back on the table to wait.

CHAPTER 15

Elle felt heavy. There was pain all through her chest and arm, and she had a headache. Her eyesight was blurry, and she was thirsty as all hell, but some of the fog was clearing. She was in post-surgery recovery. Elle glanced around, and the pain in her head increased with her efforts. A medic came over and told her to take it slow. Elle managed to croak out that she was thirsty, and the medic got her water. She took several sips, and thanked the medic as she laid her head back down on the pillow. They took her vitals and told her they would be back shortly to check on her, but to take it easy until the effects of the anesthetic wore off completely.

Elle was vaguely aware of time passing with her senses so dulled. When the medic returned, she felt more coherent. The pain was not going anywhere anytime soon; otherwise, Elle felt more like herself. From the sounds coming from outside of her room, she could tell that it was likely early the next morning, Friday. She had dozed on and off and felt she was ready to take her IVs for a stroll and use the bathroom.

When she came back to her bed, she found her team waiting. She caught the nervous look on their faces before they tried to mask them.

Eve smiled widely. "You look great, Elle, the medic said the surgery went off without a hitch and that you're recovering well so far."

Elle was on alert, and she sat down to better prepare herself for whatever they were hiding. The medics had already told her that she was a low risk for post-op complications, and she felt fine. So, they couldn't have information about her condition that would worry them. That left only one possibility; something had gone wrong with the mission.

"Okay, guys, just spit it out. What happened and how bad is it?"

They shifted uncomfortably.

Eve and Jack looked at Tex. "Nothing happened, Elle... yet. It's what's about to happen."

"What the hell does that mean?"

"Other than you getting shot, your plans seem to working out exactly as you predicted. Those bastards are at each other's throats, and things are getting nasty in their ranks. The media, intel community; and the Agency is going nuts over the upheaval in Daesh, too.

No one seems to have any idea what caused the infighting, but now everyone is trying to figure out what is going to happen next."

"That still doesn't answer my question, and stalling isn't helping my blood pressure."

Tex took a deep breath and looked at Eve and Jack. "Could you give us the room guys?"

Now Elle was on full alert.

As soon as they were gone, Tex said, "We got a message from the Agency this morning. We've been ordered to delay our departure from Baghdad."

It was a good thing Elle was sitting down, and that they had turned the sound off on her monitor; because all the alarms would have sounded at once. She was royally pissed. "Fuck that. Just because I'm wounded, it's no reason for them to butt in and—"

"It's not because of your wound, Elle," Tex interrupted. "It's because they have new information on one of our targets, and we've been ordered to eliminate them before we leave."

That didn't help ease her anger. If anything, it incensed her more. *How dare they interfere in my work again!* It was beyond unacceptable, and she considered telling them to go fuck themselves, that she would not work this way.

Tex seemed to read her mind. "I don't think they were intending to interfere, but they had credible information that was time critical. They probably thought you would want to adjust given the situation."

Elle was still seething, but she managed to say, "What information?" through gritted teeth.

"Uday Sata, Cleric, and Number 5 on your list. He's going to be in Baghdad tomorrow night for an emergency meeting of Daesh members in response to the turmoil. We have his bed down location as well as the location of the meeting. The information came from the same source who gave us Number 1, so the information has been deemed credible. This is a perfect opportunity to take him out. No one could see you wanting to pass up on the information just because it messed with your plans."

"They expect me to pull this off with such a short timeline after being wounded? How kind of them." Elle grumbled.

"They don't, Elle. I told them about the wound, and they modified the orders." Tex shifted uncomfortably. Again.

She looked at him with irritated expectation.

He finally blurted, "I've been cleared to take out the target in your absence."

Elle, rocked by the revelation, told herself that it was because of the insult of being passed over so casually, but that wasn't it. Her stomach churned and she felt bile rise in her throat. She wanted blood, but her rage was at her superiors, and herself. Angry for being responsible for putting Tex in the line of fire. It was bad enough to mess with her plans and efforts, but to mess with her team was unforgivable. The situation felt wrong to her on multiple levels, and her emotions were zinging out of control. "No fucking way. This is bullshit, and they can go to hell."

Tex looked agitated by her response, but kept his voice reasonable. "I know it's not ideal for you, but it's a completely logical option. I'm more than capable to take this guy out, and you can heal and get ready for the next phase."

He was handling her, being deferential because of her injury. It pissed her off even more. "You want to be a mindless mercenary for hire, do it elsewhere. As long as you work with me, we do things my way. You either get onboard with that or you can go."

"Go to hell, Elle. I follow your lead, your orders, and watch your back, but it doesn't make a difference. I'm your second-in-command, not some rookie."

"You were hired for a purpose. I don't care about what you want. You have a problem with your role in my operations—"

"My role?!?" Tex exploded "Fuck you, Elle. I was hired because I'm just as capable as you for this and now that fact is being pushed in your face. You want to get all butt hurt about it, fine. I'm apparently nothing to you but a whipping boy, to serve you at your whim. Fuck that. I've got a job to do. Once it's done, I'm gone. Consider this my notice." With that, he turned and left.

Her mind and her emotions were reeling. *What the hell just happened?* Her anger was instantly squelched, and she felt ill and faint. It had to be because of the injury. She felt tears burning her eyes, and she started shaking. *What is wrong with me?* Why had she lashed out like that? Had he really just quit? Was he really going to go out on this mission without her? Her breathing was coming in shallow gasps, her vision sharpened in an odd way, and time seemed to slow. She might be having an anxiety attack.

Eventually, Elle became aware that she wasn't alone anymore. Eve stood in the room looking shocked and uncertain. It was so completely out of character for Elle to break down like this that it stunned Eve into inaction; she just stood there, silently. Elle felt shame, embarrassment, and confusion all at the same time. She needed to get herself pulled together and her emotions back in check. It was essential that she get things back to the way they were supposed to be.

After a few minutes of deep breathing and forcing her mind back into focus, she finally felt like she could deal with Eve and what had happened. Elle sat up and steeled herself. All she could think to say was, "I'm okay now."

Eve's lips were pursed and her brows were drawn together in worry, but she didn't argue. She just nodded and sat down on the corner of the bed. "The doctor said that your surgery went well, and that he isn't anticipating any long-term impact."

"They told me, and I'm supposed to remain under observation for the next twenty-four hours. But why do I get the feeling that's not what you were going to tell me?" Eve shifted uncomfortably. "Just go ahead and say it, Eve, I'm not going to like it any more later than I am now."

"When the new orders came, and they heard that you were down for a while, they gave Tex the order to continue on without you." She paused, and Elle waited to hear the rest. "Jack and I have been ordered to support the mission."

Elle felt sick again. They were taking her whole team? Her jaw clenched, and she had to remind herself to breathe. She took a few minutes to make certain she was under control before she responded. "What time is his mission going?"

"We just got the orders and wanted to come see you first, so we haven't had a chance to start the mission planning. But the target is supposed to be at the meeting at 2130 tomorrow."

"Where is the meeting?"

"It's in a neighborhood in south western Baghdad, just outside the city proper."

Elle forced herself to sort out the facts of the situation and take her emotional reactions out of it. She knew she was not functioning at 100 percent, but she was struggling to come to grips with the idea that she was not viewed as capable of executing this mission. Or more to the heart of it, that she was viewed as replaceable. That thought was complicated by her anger at the changes pushed on her team by her boss. This mission just went radically out of her control, and she was not comfortable with that at all.

As much as she wanted to ignore the reality of what was happening, her reaction and treatment of Tex was wrong. He was capable, and she had not been fair to him. She had attacked him in anger, over her loss of control and fear that he would be hurt executing something that wasn't anticipated. How was she going to fix this? Could she? Tex was a proud man, and this was going to happen with or without her involvement. At least with her participation, he stood a better chance of succeeding. But, would he allow her to help after what had happened?

Elle sighed audibly. "Eve, go do what you need to do to help Tex prepare. I want to support in any way I can. Please ask Tex to come back to see me when he can."

Eve smiled at her kindly and nodded. "Want me to bring you anything?"

Elle looked around and found her iPod on the table next to the bed. "If I could get a change of clothes, the charger for my iPod, and a book, that would be perfect."

"No problem. Just try and get some rest, Elle. You really need to just worry about taking care of yourself right now. We've got everything covered until you get back."

Elle inwardly winced but knew Eve was right. How could she think so highly of her team and their capabilities one minute, but doubt them the second she wasn't the lead? It was selfish and irrational, and it may have cost her one of them already. She expected them to trust her without question, but she hadn't been able to give a fraction of that trust back to Tex when it mattered. She'd failed them, and it may have ripped her team apart just because she was afraid. That fact was a punch to the gut.

Eve returned with the requested items, and a blanket that she must have gotten from one of the vendors on base in an attempt to make Elle's stay more comfortable. She came back at meal times, too, just to make certain that Elle was getting fed properly. But, as the day continued, Tex didn't come back. Jack came with Eve during dinner and looked extremely uncomfortable, but he was trying to be supportive. They both made every effort to try and be upbeat and talk about non-pertinent things during the visit. But, Elle saw the shadow of worry in their eyes, and it made things worse. Elle didn't ask about the mission; she didn't want to put them in the middle of what was happening between her and Tex. It wouldn't be fair, and it would only cause more harm.

After they left her that night, she read for a while to keep herself distracted. She was exhausted. The trauma from the injury and the blood loss had taken a toll. Rationally, she knew that sleep was the number one thing she needed; but didn't think she would be able to. She heard a tentative knock on the door and granted entrance hoping that Tex had finally come back. She was surprised to see Julian walk in with some small books in hand.

"Looks like they took good care of you. How are you feeling?"

"Tired and sore. But mostly just sick of being in here."

"Yeah, I'm the same way. I hate hospital stays." He approached her bedside and handed her the comic books.

Her mouth curled up in a half smile when she saw what they were. *The Archie's?*

"I can't explain it, but when I was a kid my mom would buy me an Archie comic every time I was sick, and somehow it made things better. Over the years, I discovered they seemed to help when you're trapped in hospital beds, too. So, I keep a few around just in case. Thought I would offer their services to you," he said with a smile.

"Thanks, I appreciate it. I'm willing to give almost anything a try at this point."

"How long are they going to keep you here?"

"Until the morning. I don't foresee them keeping me any longer. It was a through and through."

"Anything break?"

"Nicked a bone, but overall it was a good wound."

"Guess that means it's going to be a while before a rematch." He said with a grin. "I'm still willing to give you some pointers whenever you're ready."

Even injured her body still reacted to him. "I'll keep that in mind. It'll be a little while before I could get back on the mat, but, until then, I suppose I'll just have to fight southpaw."

"Something tells me you'd do exactly that."

Elle was certain he meant that as a compliment. His body language was relaxed and he seemed genuine, but there was an air about him that told her he was capable of handling anything. It was an interesting puzzle. Who was he really, and was he a threat? If he was a threat, why did she feel so drawn to him? "Did you want to sit down?"

"I would, but I need to go. My team is going out tonight, and I have to get my gear prepped. Just wanted to swing by and say thanks."

Elle cocked her head in confusion. "Thanks for what?"

"It's always refreshing to work with professionals. It reminds me they still exist and that not everyone is here for the future movie rights," he quipped.

She laughed. "In that case, you're welcome."

Julian inclined his head to her and started to leave. He stopped when he got to the door and said, "I'm glad that you're doing okay. If you ever need another addition to your team, please keep me in mind." Then added a teasing, "Even if it's just to help coach you in boxing."

Elle's laughter followed him out of the room. When the door closed, she felt better than before; although, a small part of her wished Julian would come back. It was the first time she could remember wanting someone's company instead of solitude. Elle picked up one of the comic books and began to read. She found herself enjoying the antics of the teenagers in the stories. They were comical but still managed to have a small-town wholesomeness that was a pleasant departure from her reality. It really did lift her spirits and provide a great distraction from being in the hospital. Strange, it was such a small thing, but she couldn't deny that it worked.

After she finished the comic, she turned out the lights, pulled on her headphones, and tried to get some sleep. After a few minutes, she felt her muscles fully relax and she was able to clear her mind. She finally drifted off feeling calm and hopeful.

CHAPTER 16

The following morning, Elle showered and changed into the clothes Eve brought the day previous. She was more than ready to get out of the hospital, and was fighting impatience waiting for her discharge. She was lying on the bed reading the second comic book when there was a knock on the door. Anticipating the doctor, Elle got to her feet and was taken off guard when Tex walked in.

She had convinced herself that he wasn't going to come or give her the chance to try and make things right, so she had forced herself to stop thinking about it. Now as he stood in front of her, she found herself off balance and at a loss for words.

He stood just inside the door and looked at her for a long moment before he said, "You look ready to go."

Elle found her voice, but it cracked from the effort of trying to sound casual, "Just waiting for the green light from the doctor."

Tex nodded, but then just stood there, waiting for her to talk.

She felt anxious, and that made it hard for her to get her bearings. Eventually, she shifted her weight, straightened her shoulders; and jumped in. "I wasn't fair to you yesterday and said things that were flat-out wrong. I'm sorry. I have no excuse for what I did...and I hope that you will withdraw your notice."

He cocked his head and arched an eyebrow. He wasn't going to let her off the hook so easily.

Elle took a deep breath and growled a little when she exhaled, "I do value you, more than I ever tell you, and I'm an ass because of that. You are capable, and talented, and I hold you back. It's completely irrational and unfounded."

Elle tried to be as straight forward and succinct as possible, but she could feel her emotions welling up. She noticed some shaking in her hands and legs, and her throat felt like it was constricting; her lower lip kept trembling of its own accord. She tried to rein her body back under control, but it wasn't listening. It made her feel worse. She was flailing and she didn't like the feeling. It was as if her brain had lost a battle and her emotions now had complete control of her body.

Tex looked at her a long time. "What's going on, Elle, seriously, you've been off lately. You need to level with me."

She didn't want to admit to anything she had been struggling with, but she knew instinctively that this was a pivotal moment for her and Tex. "I honestly don't know. As a rule, emotions are not something I feel, let alone deal with. I've been getting overwhelmed by things that I just don't know how to process, and I don't understand why they're happening. My focus has been split, my thoughts haven't been strictly rational, and my body seems to have betrayed me." She flopped down on the bed in exasperation with herself and the situation. "I must be losing my mind or something else is wrong with me."

He studied her face. "What happened yesterday?"

Elle grimaced. She had known the question would come up eventually, but she still didn't want to talk about it. She swallowed her ego and said, "Mostly, I was afraid."

"Of what?"

"I was afraid for you, and the loss of control over the situation."

His features darkened.

She knew he was taking that as confirmation that she didn't think him capable of doing anything other than being her assistant. So, she told him what she finally had to admit to herself, "What if it's another trap? Like your first assignment. I couldn't handle losing you, Mike." She couldn't look at him after admitting that, but she could see his arms drop to his sides and his posture shift. She had taken him by surprise.

She felt vulnerable and anxious, but she pressed on. If their relationship was over, then he deserved to hear the truth. "I've never really connected with anyone, my parents included. I liked them and thought that they were good people, but that was as far as I ever got before they died. Everyone else in my life hasn't been worth keeping around, and I enjoy my solitude. But then you and Eve and Jack were dropped in my path. You're the closest approximation of family for me. I think that has brought on an onslaught of emotions that I didn't even know I was capable of feeling. I was confused, unsettled, and fought it because it was wrecking the way I do business right in the middle of an op. The timing couldn't have been worse, so I thought I could force myself to stop. I failed. I acted the way I did because the idea of you being in the crosshairs because of me...is unacceptable. Rational thought be damned. I felt like my guts were ripping themselves out of my body. I couldn't handle it, and I lashed out."

She sat, staring at the floor for what seemed like an eternity. When Tex finally moved, Elle had no idea how much time had passed or what to expect. He grabbed the chair and dragged it over to her and sat down. He sighed loudly and said, "Well, you sure know how to take the fight right out of a man. I was determined to give you hell for that bullshit, but that would be a low blow at this point. He leaned forward, putting his elbows on his knees so that she was forced to look him in the face.

"So, you have some human qualities after all…gonna take some getting used to. But your secret is safe with me, Mama."

Elle teared up at the endearment and turned away, blinking rapidly to keep them from falling down her face.

"I suppose I can move past the affront to my manhood and extend an olive branch. But, from here on out, we're partners. It's still your lead, but I'm done playing secretary."

She snorted and smiled but still didn't feel in control enough to look at him. She just nodded.

Tex grabbed her hand and gave it a slight squeeze, trying to be encouraging. "How long before you can get out of here?"

Tex was letting her off too easily, but she took the opportunity to try and regain her equilibrium. "The Doc was supposed to be here any time now. I thought you were him when you knocked."

"Well, let's go see what the holdup is. Get your shit together. We've got work to do."

Elle grabbed her belongings and they left.

The medic they ran into didn't look pleased that she had left before she was discharged, but he wisely kept his mouth shut. He brought the doctor to them and, after a few admonitions and the issuing of instructions for aftercare and recuperation—that she intended to mostly ignore—they were on their way.

"I hope you got some rest on your little vacation, Elle, because you've got some catching up to do." Tex chastised her.

"Well, the cabana boy was late with my drinks, and the food sucked, but I did still manage to get a nap in poolside."

"Slacker."

Making their way back to the office, Elle could see where they had begun to pack but had stopped because of the new orders. Eve and Jack looked up when they walked in, both had a look of apprehension on their faces, waiting to see where things stood with all of them.

Tex puffed out his chest, did a little arrogant swagger, and told them in his best pirate imitation, "There be a new order around here now, and it's not for the faint of heart. The Captain is taking us on as full partners. We all know exactly what that means and the possible messiness involved. So, what say you? You in or out?"

Eve and Jack looked at each other and then at Elle, trying to figure out whether Tex was serious or if this was some kind of joke. They waited for her reaction.

She needed to stop fighting with herself. She couldn't deny or control the emotions; the best option was to stop trying. *To hell with it.* How could she face being shot without batting an eye but have issues with talking to the people she valued most? She took a deep breath and said, "I suppose the lunatic over here has a point. You all put a lot into what we do, and I trust you more than anyone else. The job isn't easy, and it can take a moral and emotional toll if you don't fully invest in the idea that, in this work, the end justifies the means. Murder, sabotage, espionage are just a few examples of our everyday tasks. It's savage, but I do it because I know that my end game is to disrupt and eventually destroy Daesh. I have no issues with getting my hands dirty to do that. But, I have to remind you about the incident with the video of the woman's punishment. And, Jack, I know you saw what I did to Number 1. I won't have any time to deal with a moral crisis while I'm working. You need to be certain you can handle the strain."

Tex looked pleased and watched Eve and Jack expectantly.

Surprisingly, it was Jack who spoke up first, "We've known what you've been doing ever since we started working with you, Elle. It's just difficult to reconcile it sometimes with the idea that we are the good guys. My head understands, but my guts recoil. I guess I have this childish idea of what it means to be the hero...."

Eve echoed Jack, "I always had this sinking feeling, like somehow if we didn't do everything honorably, we were making things worse. That we were putting more evil into the world, instead of taking it out." She paused then added, "But, I never doubted that you were doing what you thought best, and it's not possible to argue with the results you've gotten. I can't promise that I won't still have struggles, but I can promise I'll do my best to not let it impact my work, and I'll support you no matter what."

Jack nodded. "I'm in. Both Marvel and DC went dark to save the medium, so I can handle anything you throw at me."

Everyone started laughing. He even chuckled and blushed.

Elle felt a twinge of unease, but mostly she was honored by their trust. "Alright then. I know we have work to do, so can you bring me up to speed on Tex's mission?"

They seemed taken off guard by her question, so Tex jumped in, "Elle and I will go in together on this one. I'll need her to be my eyes and ears while I'm in the building. Let's get her up to speed and refine the plan to include her as overwatch."

Eve moved over to her desk and pulled up an overhead image of what appeared to be an apartment complex. "Here is the target location. The meeting is going down at 2130 in this southern building. The target is allegedly staying in apartment 214 afterward, which is on the second floor."

Elle studied the image of a large apartment complex with a main entrance, exit, and no surrounding structures. It would make the chances of a surreptitious approach almost impossible. The location was a nightmare for any force that wasn't at least one hundred strong with tanks and helicopters. No wonder they'd selected this spot for the meeting and bed down location. If they were not extremely careful, this would be disastrous.

"What's your game plan?"

"The location is an assault team's nightmare but, if you can get inside, its perfect for sniper operations or a more unconventional approach. We're going to be using a foot ingress from about five miles away. The storm that's coming this way is going to have an impact, but it will also limit visibility and make it possible for two people on foot to get to the eastern building. From there, I'll need to move around to the southern building to gain entry and take out the target. I'll need you to be my backup, and give me overwatch from one of the other structures. The northern building seems to have the best field of view, and give me as much situational awareness as possible," Tex told her.

She felt a chill go down her spine. Elle didn't like this op, and she couldn't be sure why. She was reluctant to say anything and risk them thinking it was her being overly emotional again, but it wasn't that. She was sure something was off. "Do we have eyes overhead? Have we been able to get a look at traffic patterns around the buildings?"

"Our information is limited. But, from the looks we've been able to get, it's a low activity location. It appears that there are doors at the front and back of each building, and that the fronts are more heavily utilized since they're closest to the parking areas. The lot seems to only ever be about a quarter full. But, there's no telling how many people are inside squatting. There are also fire escapes at each end," Eve informed her.

"What direction is the wind and weather pattern moving tonight?"

"It's coming out of the west and heading southeast. The forecasts are indicating that the worst of it will be over the target around the time of the meeting. Visibility will be extremely low; even ambient light will have difficulty aiding your efforts."

Her uneasy feeling grew, but she wasn't certain how to articulate it. "This location, plus the weather, gives this op an extremely low probability for success. How long did the source say the target would be bedding down at the location?"

"We only have tonight. He allegedly leaves for morning prayer and won't be returning," Tex said.

"And, we're certain of the source's information?" Elle asked, trying to figure out why she was unsettled.

"As certain as we can be. The source gave us the information about the first target, so he has the credibility and a proven track record at this point."

Her pulse spiked. There it was. That's what was eating at her. "What do we know about the source?"

"Not much, just the usual broad strokes. Mid-level extremist directly involved in Daesh operations."

"Any reason why they think he's giving these guys up?"

Tex raised an eyebrow. "They didn't say. Probably money. Does it matter? The information was good. Isn't that the important part?"

He was right, at least for what they were doing. Elle wasn't running the source gathering the information, she was just acting on it. So, why did she feel as though that was a problem? "I don't like it, Tex. Something about this is making me uneasy. I can't tell you any more than that because I still can't figure out what's bothering me so much, but it needs to be said."

"So, what are you suggesting?" Tex asked.

She looked him in the eye. "If it were up to me, I would call this off based on the weather alone, but it's not my mission, and I'm going to follow your lead. Whatever you choose, I will back you."

Tex looked at her for a moment before turning back to the screen, "If we don't try, we lose this chance and risk them messing with us again sooner rather than later. Worst-case, we go in, and we're blown before we get there, or something fucks us, and we miss the opportunity. I say we push this as far as we can and get it done and over with so we can get back on track."

Elle pursed her lips, but nodded, "Alright, let's talk details and work out where you want me to post up."

He looked at Eve and Jack and said, "Give us everything you've got on the layout of the structure, the target, and the possible participants in the meeting. Jack, I need whatever schematics you can find. Eve, please check the routes on the way in, and keep an eye on the storm." He turned to Elle. "Let's get to work."

CHAPTER 17

L ater that evening as Elle and Tex prepped their gear and got ready to step off; they ran over the details of the plan. Other than the complication of the weather, the operation was about as simple as it got. Regardless of that fact, Elle's anxiety only grew as time passed. She couldn't shake the feeling that something was wrong, and they should abort the mission. She said as much to Tex, and he tried to reassure her. She could see it written all over his face that he thought she was worried about him. Assuming that she was still struggling with her revelation from earlier, and this was fallout from seeing him running an op in less-than-ideal conditions. She didn't blame him, and she doubted herself a little, too.

They would be taking the car to an area to the east of the complex and hiking in from there dressed as locals. The schematics Jack had located were recent and showed that Apartment 214 faced the main parking area. Elle was to set up in position on the northern building to provide overwatch for Tex. He was going to enter the building and go to 214 to wait on the target to return from the meeting. Elle would be his eyes, cueing him if there were any indications that the apartment was already occupied and calling out movement for his situational awareness. She was also critical to making certain he got out of the building without running into a lot of people who might wonder why he was there. For his part, he was taking a page out of Elle's book and going in for the quiet kill. That should buy them the time they would need to get out of dodge before anyone discovered the body.

Elle placed her rifle in her customized case; and followed Tex out to the Ops center to get briefed. It was strange; they had prepared for this mission exactly the same, but it still felt different. Tex had been the lead on the planning, but Elle had been there with him through all the final phases. It was different going into this as partners; and not in superior-subordinate roles. Was that why she was uneasy? Could she be having that much inner turmoil over this change?

Eve launched into her brief, and gave them the latest information on the routes they would be taking and on the weather. There had been an IED strike earlier on their primary route, so they would need to be careful.

Chances were high that the route would remain clear since the Iraqis would be on alert; and on the lookout for someone trying to take advantage of the disturbed earth to plant another IED. The strike had likely been targeting the Iraqi Security Forces anyway, which would make them more vigilant.

As for the weather, it was looking uglier as they got closer to stepping off. By the time Elle and Tex would be making their walk back to the car, they would be getting hammered by wind and rain. Rain, and the desert did not get along. They'd have to keep a constant watch for lightning strikes and flash flooding in the dry wadis they would have to cross. The less time they spent on target, the better. Getting out was looking to be the most dangerous part of the operation.

When they walked out of their building, a swift wind kicked dirt up all around them, and Elle lifted her hand to shield her eyes. She winced, as the pain in her shoulder reminded her that she wasn't at full strength. The doctor would have likely shit a brick if he knew what she was doing; but, there was no way in hell Tex was going out on this alone. She got into the car and started to put in her iPod when she noticed one there already. She quirked an eyebrow at Tex and nodded toward the device.

He smiled. "My op, my music."

She rolled her eyes and tried to hide her smile. "It better not be boy bands or else you might not make it back tonight."

"You cretin. Have you no appreciation for the finer things in life?"

"Guess I'm just not that cultured," she shot back.

They left the base and made good time to their starting point. Tex played some newer hard rock that Elle enjoyed, and they both got mentally prepared for what was in front of them. As they drove into the storm, it got progressively worse. Eve's weather report had been spot on, which meant the longer they were out, the worse it was going to get for them. If they were very lucky, they would beat the rain. Looking at the terrain, Elle's gut knotted a little with the anticipation of being caught out in the storm. There was a large wadi with smaller branches that bisected the area they had to cross. If the rain came down in the predicted deluge, it wouldn't be long at all before flash flooding became a reality instead of a possibility.

Tex must have been having similar thoughts because he broke the silence with, "Let's get moving so we can get out of here as soon as possible. Hopefully, those bastards aren't operating on 'Inshallah' time tonight." She agreed. A lot of the locals tended to do things in their own time and insisted that it would happen "when God willed it," instead of just admitting that they didn't care about meeting deadlines.

Once out of the car, they got their bearings and started the long walk. It would take them about two hours to make the hike, and they would be in the open the entire time. They hoped the weather and the time of day would limit the possibility that anyone would be paying attention, and, if anyone did glance at them, they would assume they were locals going to the apartment complex to get out of the weather or squat in one of the unoccupied spaces.

The terrain wasn't difficult, but it was uneven, and the branches of the large wadi that crossed their path every so often made the footing questionable at times. They did their best to try and put the landscape to memory so that when they made the return trek in the dark, in the rain, and with NVGs on, they would have some frame of reference. That may help keep them from breaking something or falling into rushing water. The wind kept kicking up sand, and the waning light made it difficult to maintain their pace at times, but they pushed on.

When they finally saw the buildings in the distance, it was almost a relief until Elle's internal warning system started going off again. "Tex, I need you to promise me that you'll keep your head on a swivel as we do this and that you won't argue with me if I tell you to bounce."

Tex started to argue, probably more out of habit than anything else, but the tone of her voice was alerting to him. "Talk to me, Elle. What's really going on here?"

"I can't place it. But, over the years I've learned to trust my instincts. My emotions have jacked things up for me this week, but my instincts have never let me down. I'm going to level with you and tell you that I can't be sure that this isn't somehow connected to my fear of something happening to you, but I am 100 percent certain that something in my gut is screaming at me. If I'm wrong, so be it, but if I'm not—we need to be ready."

"Okay, we'll do this by the numbers. You're my overwatch, and if you see something you don't like, we abort, and I won't question you. We'll debrief when we get back and come up with our next move. But, you've got to promise me that you won't get twitchy just because I'm in there and you aren't."

"I won't lie. I hate that you're going to be in that building. But I take watching your back very seriously. I'm not going to allow my ego to distract me from that. Besides, I'll be prone on the roof in this shit. I'll mostly be cussing at you for being warm and dry while I get hammered by sand and rain."

He laughed. "Suck it up, princess, you're going soft."

"Remind me to kick your ass when we get back."

"Bring it, gimpy. I know your right cross is your best punch, and you're not going to be doing that anytime soon."

"You're always underestimating me. One of these days..." Elle let the sentence trail off into silence. They needed to get back into character in their stance, just in case someone was looking their way.

Elle dropped a couple of steps behind Tex and hunched her shoulders to present a smaller, more submissive posture. They started pointing out features of the apartment complex and surrounding terrain to make certain they both had the same information to work from. The buildings had been well built; but not maintained in years. The exterior was mostly intact, but you could see that chunks of concrete had fallen out in a few places, likely from rocket or mortar attacks. The fire escapes were rusted but looked solid. As they got closer to the buildings, they saw bullet holes and windows that had been broken and covered with cardboard. The back of the eastern building was right in front of them. The rear door seemed dented and a little off its hinges and there weren't many windows with light coming from them.

Once they reached the back of the eastern building, they did a final communications check and separated, Tex headed south to use the back door of the southern building, Elle, to the north to get to the roof of the northern building. Tex would wait until she was in position and could give him an idea of what the current situation was before he entered the building, just in case he needed to change tactics to ensure surreptitious entry.

Elle rounded the corner and saw the fire escape on the side of the building she needed. She cautiously scanned the surroundings and the windows to make sure nobody was watching her. Elle wore all black, and, if she was careful, her movements would not draw attention in the storm. She studied the stairs of the fire escape and they looked capable of supporting her weight, but she would have to vault over some makeshift barricades to gain access to each of the floors. Usually, it wouldn't even give her pause but, with one shoulder down, it might be a challenge. The weather didn't help either.

She moved around the corner and walked directly for the fire escape. She adopted her hobbled, slouched posture, wanting to appear as pathetic and uninteresting as possible—just another poor woman trying to find a place out of the storm. The weather was picking up, so no one was waiting around outside. She kept an eye on the windows, watching for any indications of being observed. While she couldn't see anything that caught her attention, the hair on the back of her neck stood on end. She felt eyes. Elle kept watching all around; but did not see anything. The only explanation was that someone in one of the darkened rooms was looking out their window. She hoped she looked as nonthreatening and pathetic as intended.

When she reached the fire escape, the shadows closest to the building helped cloak her presence and to allow more freedom of movement. She needed to move quickly. The longer she took to get into position, the longer Tex was waiting in limbo. She vaulted over the first barricade using her good arm and stepped as lightly on the stairs as possible.

They were a little rickety, but they held her weight. Elle hoped that once she got to high ground, she would be able to finally settle her nerves. She took the next two barricades in stride and paused at the one blocking the top of the building so she could be sure it was clear. There was a door in the center of the roof that allowed the occupants of the building access. There were also several water tanks and multiple old mattresses from where people had chosen to sleep on the roof to get some relief on hot days.

She held still for several moments, but it appeared the weather had helped to ensure she would be alone on the roof tonight. She crossed the final barricade and moved to set up so that she could give Tex the information he needed. She checked in with him over the radio. "Setting up now, so far no movement."

"Copy all. Door was secured with a chain and padlock. It's disabled now. Standing by," he replied.

Elle pulled out her rifle and used an old chair to help her overlook the parapet. The weapon went automatically to her right shoulder, and she paid for that moment of muscle memory. Breathing through some pain, she tried to decide how she wanted to proceed. Should she switch shoulders? She was a good weak side shot, but she was right-eye dominant. Despite the discomfort, she decided to stick with her right side. Since overwatch was her mission, she needed her eyes more than her ability to shoot. Once she was in position, she surveyed the area. It was quiet. She checked Room 214 and found lights on but no covering on the windows. That gave her pause. Shouldn't there at least be a makeshift curtain?

She checked the lot and then her watch. There were numerous cars parked near the southern building, and the meeting should have started. Where were the guards? Were they that complacent, or was the meeting not happening?

"It's quiet. Too quiet. I don't see any movement anywhere, and there are no guards stationed around the building. This doesn't feel right."

"Do you have line of sight into the apartment?"

"Yes, this location is perfect for overwatch. There are no window covers. It looks empty, but the lights are on."

The silence was palpable. Elle surmised that Tex was starting to feel the wrongness of the situation. She continued to look around the area as she waited for him to process what she'd said.

"Do you think the intel is bad? Could the meeting have changed because of the weather?" he asked.

"I don't know, but we need to either get you in that room or we need to abort now."

There was another pause, and then he said, "What do you think?"

"I say we abort. This feels all kinds of wrong, and what I'm seeing doesn't support the intel."

As if on cue, the front door of the southern building opened, and a group of men walked out. "We've got action out front, eight males. One is in custody." As she focused in on the group, she noted the features of the man who was bound in the middle; it was the target. "Number 5 is the prisoner, and he looks shocked and confused." She scanned the rest of the group and saw that she recognized another one. "Our Number 3 seems to be running this little mob." She watched him saunter in front of 5 and face him. Elle knew what was about to happen before the gun even appeared. She watched as he pulled out a pistol and put a bullet between 5's eyes.

The body had just hit the deck when 3 turned and looked up at her.

Her blood went cold. She didn't hear anything but felt the attack coming and reacted on instinct. She rolled out of the chair to her left, and used her momentum to help her get further away while turning to face the threat. There were four men on the roof with her now— all heavily armed. Elle had a fraction of a second to decide what to do. She raised her hands and made like she was going to drop her weapon. She needed them to believe they had intimidated her into submission with their numbers. Tex was frantic in her ear, trying to get a situation report after the gunshot. Just as she was about to drop her weapon, she dove across some mattresses and kept rolling until she was behind a water tank.

It was plastic, so it didn't give her any cover, but she only needed a second of concealment. "It's a set up! Abort, abort, abort! Get the fuck out of here, Mike, don't argue, just move! The team needs you."

She barely registered that Tex was screaming at her over the pain shooting through her right side and the sounds of her pursuers. She grabbed her SIG and fired at the first man who rounded the corner; the recoil sent new pain through her. She shot twice at his chest and twice at his head automatically. He wore body armor, but it didn't stop the two to the head, and he went down hard.

The next thing she knew, her left leg went out from under her; she didn't hear anything over the blood rushing through her ears. The force of the impact and the all-too-familiar pain left no doubt that she'd gotten shot. Unlike his rash comrade, one of the men had gone around the roof access and used the only cover available to line up on her. That told her a lot. These men were pros, mercenaries hired for a job. The man she shot may have been fooled by her act, but the others were not. Reality crushed her. They meant business and, apparently, this was a capture mission because there was no way anyone trained should have missed her from that distance.

Pure adrenaline allowed her to move through the pain. She aimed to take out the shooter, but a large boot kicked the gun out of her hand with such force it must have broken bone. She couldn't differentiate from that pain and the pain the jarring impact had on her shoulder. Her vision tunneled, and she saw stars. Then, her equilibrium disappeared for a moment, and that was all it took. Time slowed, she heard the desperate note in Tex's voice—demanding that she tell him she was alright. The last thing she saw before everything went black was a dark-skinned man rearing back to deliver a knock-out punch.

CHAPTER 18

Elle became aware of two things: pain and cold. She instinctively fought waking up because it was only going to get worse if she did; her subconscious and body wanted to avoid reality. But then her mind clicked into focus through the pain, and she remembered the roof. Everything hurt; worse than anything she had experienced previously, and she tried to sort through the pain to determine how bad the damage might be. She was naked, shivering uncontrollably, which was exasperating her awkward position and intensifying the pain of her injuries.

Her arms were tied tightly behind her, and she was sitting hunched forward in a chair. There were ropes around her calves that kept her bound to the chair with her knees apart, and she was blind folded. Her shoulder felt like it had been ripped in half, and her right hand felt bruised and swollen. She tried to move it and found she could not move two of her fingers. Her head was pounding like someone was beating her with a hammer, and her face felt battered. She tasted blood in her mouth, a lot of it, which meant some of her teeth were probably loose. There was material on her left leg just above her knee. It felt like the bandage was cutting off all circulation, causing muscle spasms and lightning bolts of electricity to run up her body. They must have applied a pressure dressing to stop the bleeding.

Which meant, they wanted her alive.

She sat quietly for a moment, breathing, forcing herself to use her nose and ears to gain any information about where she was and if she was alone. Silence and dust greeted her. Next, she tested the bonds holding her, fighting through the agony movement caused, and was rewarded with a little give in her right wrist. She was very thirsty, cold, and in addition to blood, tasted something chemical in her mouth. Elle would put money on blood loss and drugs being the cause of that. The wound care she'd received was strictly to keep her alive, and they wanted her extremely vulnerable—meaning she wasn't going to be alive for long. There was a silent countdown on her life. She was going to have to find a way out while she still had some strength left. The longer she was here, the further her already-slim chance of escaping slipped away.

Elle heard approaching footsteps, and a bolt being unlatched before a door creaked open. She forced herself to hunch forward again, even though her body protested intensely. There were some shuffling sounds, a soft thud, a zipper opening, some clicking and tapping, and the sound of metal scraping metal. Elle felt bile rise in her throat and fought it back down; they were setting up a camera. She was about to become propaganda.

Voices moved towards her, men, speaking in authoritative tones. Once they were close enough for her to make out what they were saying, she heard them boasting about their great victory and their perfect plan. She guessed that three more men entered the room. She heard some more movement, and then ice-cold water hit her unexpectedly. She couldn't control her body's reaction, and the jolt was excruciating on her battered condition. Her breath came in ragged gasps as she panted in pain. The men laughed, and one of them ripped the blindfold off. She saw stars and the light pierced her eyes like daggers.

When her vision cleared enough to make out her surroundings, it was not inspiring. The room didn't have any windows, and looked like it may have been an old bathroom or locker room. The floor was concrete and the wall had tiles, some of which were discolored and had holes from where plumbing had been previously. There was a table, and she recognized her gear lying on top. The camera sat on a tripod, and they had a bright light hanging over her head. She kept her wits about her enough to make it look like she couldn't focus on anything and was dizzy, so she allowed her head to lull from one side to the other.

Two of the men wore tailored shirts, slacks, and leather sandals. She saw flashes of gold jewelry. The cameraman wore a tracksuit. But, it was the third man that had her worried. He had to be the bodyguard; and he looked like a man well acquainted with violence. He was a large man with a military style haircut, black tactical gear, and a stoic demeanor. After a moment, one of the well-dressed men signaled to the cameraman to start recording.

That man stepped toward her, and she recognized him. It was Number 3. He held his shoulders back and his head up as he strutted in front of the camera—all theatrics to look powerful, to make her feel pathetic. 'The Great Satan sent this lowly whore to murder our brothers in its cowardice. We captured this cow after she struck down a great cleric from the shadows while he tended to his family. We will send a powerful message back to all the Western dogs: They cannot stop the will of Allah. We will send them all screaming into the darkness." He turned and walked off camera and signaled for it to be turned off. Once the recording stopped, 3 sent the cameraman and the other man out of the room. Only the bodyguard stayed.

Number 3 pulled a chair up, lit a cigarette, and made himself comfortable. After a moment, he addressed her in English, "I did not expect a woman to be the assassin that would carry out our bidding. But, I suppose I shouldn't put anything past you Americans."

Elle remained hunched and trembled. He continued. "Tell me, how did you manage to kill the Imam? He was well guarded. And the posts were expertly created and published."

Elle's mind worked furiously, putting together the pieces from what he just said with her current situation. This asshole had to have been the source who fed them the information about the targets. It was a power play by either the Syrian based elements or by this man alone. They had used her to take out the Baghdad Imam and set her up to take the fall for the Baghdad Cleric. With those men out of the picture, he would ascend to be one of the leading religious and spiritual advisors for the group. He could craft and pass out fatwas and make so-called scholarly determinations that would be the foundation for Daesh's activity. It gave him sway over its large population of killers and the ability to drive the intentions of the group.

She wasn't going to be able to sell ignorance or weakness with this man. He already believed her to be a hired assassin. If she didn't play this just right, he would have her killed without hesitation. Elle worked up some saliva and held it in her mouth; she was gambling on her read of the situation and hoped she was right.

"I took into consideration the great service you have done for us, and I toyed with the idea of sparing your life. Of course, that isn't going to happen. But I will offer you a choice that will decide how horrible an end it will be for you. I want information, and you are going to give it to me one way or the other. The less you resist, the more merciful I will be. Defy me, and I will have you brutalized by my men until you are nothing more than a bloody piece of flesh begging for death."

Elle felt the tension rise at her silence and allowed some of the saliva to drip out of her mouth. A second later, her head was ripped up violently by her hair. She forced her muscles to stay loose and rolled her eyes back; the saliva looked like drool. Her jaw slack, she ignored the pain in her head and allowed her head to hang from the hair held by the bodyguard. She was banking on the fact that she had been drugged and had a concussion. It worked—with one serious drawback.

Number 3 cursed in Arabic, then came the first hit, a forceful slap across her face. She didn't try to slow the momentum caused by the blow and let her head whip around. Some of her hair ripped out at the roots as her head was knocked around by the force of the strike. She made her body bob and twitch as if she couldn't function properly. The next blow felt like a cane to her wounded leg. Everything went white behind her eyelids, and the scream lodged in her throat. Elle fought through and allowed herself to gurgle and shake as though the reaction was involuntary.

3 was furious. He screamed at his guard, and accused him of ruining his plans intentionally. A drugged whore was worthless to him. He needed her awake and coherent; and demanded that the guard fix this immediately. His anger was white hot, and he took it out on her again, reeling around and kicking her chair over. Elle didn't brace for the impact. She was rewarded for her convincing portrayal when Number 3 started to kick and stomp on her shoulder and in the ribs. She desperately wanted to pass out. The pain was too much. It was everywhere. Somehow, she held onto consciousness. Sheer will to survive kept her in the moment.

The bodyguard told 3 that if he continued, she was as good as dead. It bought her a reprieve. She became aware that she was breathing shallowly, making a slight, keening noise. It wasn't intentional, but it served her well. She only hoped that it didn't mean that she was further gone than she knew. The guard told 3 that her injuries had compounded the effects of the drugs they had used to keep her unconscious during transport. He suggested that they use a saline IV to push the sedatives from her system, and, if she didn't regain some coherence, then they use an amphetamine to force her awake.

The silence that followed felt like an eternity. Elle's life hinged on this moment. There was some rustling and then the men were leaving the room and shutting the door. She cautiously opened an eye after the steps faded, and saw that the room appeared empty. Hoping that 3 had nodded in consent to his guard's proposal, and that she bought herself a few moments alone, she began to reassess her situation.

Something was very wrong. It was like a part of Elle's mind had shut off. She knew she was in more pain than she had ever been before and that it should be debilitating, but it wasn't registering. *No!* Panic set in at what that could mean for her, and she had to fight to regain her focus. Permanent damage or not, it wouldn't matter if she didn't get out of there. Making her mind shift away from the terror of what an inability to detect pain meant, she told herself to embrace it since it could be the difference between life and death. She moved her head, and it responded as it should. But, she didn't feel anything.

Refusing to waste any more time on the issue, she went to work on her escape. She tested the give in the bonds holding her wrists. The curve in the chair back had prevented her hands from being crushed under her weight during the fall, but they were pinned. She looked at her legs next. They were still bound, but one looked loose. She pulled her knee toward her chest and saw it move, and the rope only caught partway. Elle started working her leg up and down the chair gradually working the rope down to her ankle. She knew it had to be causing rope burn, and that she was ripping the skin off her leg, but she kept going.

Just as she ripped her foot free, she heard footsteps approaching. Listening closely, it was only one set. There was no way to get back into the rope in time, so she positioned her leg as if it was still bound and hoped that they wouldn't notice or think it happened during her beating. The bolt pulled back, and the door opened. The footsteps were hesitant. It had to be someone who hadn't seen what 3 had done to her. The steps moved over to her and stood very close by. The light shifted as they moved to crouch over her. She smelled foul breath; then pressure on her breast.

She was being molested while they thought she was unconscious.

Rage burned in her stomach, and she wanted blood, but she tramped those feeling down to do the last thing she wanted to do. She fluttered her eyes open and saw the cameraman looking down on her, lust visible on his face. She could use that. She used broken Arabic, to say "Please…help…give…anything."

The cameraman started, and she could see the wheels turning in his head. He was trying to decide what he could get away with. She shifted her body intentionally calling attention to her breasts; and then squirming knowing it would draw his eye down the rest of her naked body. She was intentionally feeding his fantasy. Again, she said, "Give anything."

His hand went to his crotch, and he started rubbing himself, he looked pointedly at his groin and then at hers. Elle made a show of looking resigned, then moved her groin as if inviting him and repeated, "Give, anything, help, please."

The pervert looked triumphant; as if the stupid, American whore would do anything he wanted her to. He pulled his pants off and grabbed at her breasts and roughly kissed her.

She forced herself to endure it. She needed to bide her time for the perfect moment. His hand ran down to the junction between her legs, and he forced his fingers inside her. She wanted to scream, to go on the attack, but she held still for the violation. Her moment was coming, he was underestimating her, and she would make sure that it would be the last mistake of his life. He pulled back and grabbed at her hips, trying to shift her to get an angle to rape her, but she hooked her leg in such a way that the chair moved with her. His only option to get access to her would be to untie her leg. Doubt crept in behind the feverish look on his face, so Elle moved her groin suggestively and whimpered, "Please."

That did it. Overcome by lust and the conviction Elle was completely helpless, the cameraman untied the rope like a man obsessed. Focused entirely on fucking her, he didn't notice that when he moved her into position, one of her legs lined up directly under his chin. Elle put all her strength and will into the kick. She curled her toes back as far as she could, as quickly as she could. She aimed as though she was kicking through the top of his head. This hit had to count. If it didn't at least knock him out, she was doomed.

Her would-be rapist's head snapped back with such force; it didn't look real. Whether it was her desperation, the fact that she couldn't feel pain or both, she landed the kick; it worked. Blood sprayed on impact, he must have bit his tongue, and she heard a crack. His weightless body followed his head's movement, and he fell over awkwardly, landing hard on the tile floor. Silence ruled again.

Elle was lying in a weird position, but now both her legs were free, and the pervert had unbolted the door when he came in. As vile as the experience had been, she was in a much better situation than before. She focused on using her lower body to rock the chair. The momentum she created helped her roll the chair over. From there, she worked herself into a kneeling, then standing, position. On standing, her vision blurred and her head swam. She was dangerously close to passing out.

Elle used what senses she still had left to help ground her in the present. The spell passed, and she was on the move again. She shuffled over to the table, to her gear, which was arranged in an elaborate display. 3 must have been intending to use it in his propaganda video as proof of her guilt and their superiority. She angled her body and the chair to get her hand over her knife. Two of her fingers did not want to respond on her right hand, so she had to switch over to use her left. From there, she sat down in the chair to give herself a steady base and started "feeling" with the blade tip for the rope on her opposing arm.

She felt the pressure of the knife touching her skin, and tried not to think about the damage she was doing to herself. The blade was extremely sharp; it cut through flesh easily. She pushed that thought away and concentrated on escaping. She judged the distance of where the rope was on her arm and the depth of the binds and started small sawing motions. The pressure on her arm felt like it loosened, so she continued, pulling constantly against the rope to keep tension. After a couple of minutes, she felt movement. The line was fraying. She kept at it. Within moments, the rope snapped.

Elle pulled her arm free and saw blood running down it, but luckily it was a surface wound and not arterial. She reached around her back to grab the knife so she could cut her other arm free. This time she could see the rope, but still got a few scratches since she could only use her thumb and two fingers on her right hand. Once she was free of the chair, she returned to the pervert and removed his track suit. Once it was off, Elle slit his throat. He may have been dead already, but she wasn't leaving without making sure.

She dressed as quickly as she could in his clothes, trying not to gag from the stench. Elle still couldn't feel any pain, but the way her body moved left no doubt that the damage was substantial and had she been able to feel it, she wouldn't have been able to function. Time was running out. She returned to the table and put her gear back in her bag. Her radio, phone, and iPod had been smashed, but her weapons were still loaded. She put on her pack and slung her rifle. She didn't trust herself to be able to hold the long gun so she would rely on her pistols. Even shooting weak side, she had more confidence with being able to handle the SIGs. The last thing she did before she left the room was to go to the camera and remove the memory card. She snapped it in half and dropped it down an old drain in the floor.

Knowing time was running out, she paused at the door long enough to listen for any sounds that might let her know there were guards beyond it. She didn't hear anything, so she pulled the door open with her gun at the ready, and quartered the area outside the room. No one was there, and she found herself in an empty hallway with several other doors. She moved as quickly and quietly as she could, but her left leg wasn't working properly, and it was starting to give out on her. It was a risk, but she moved past each door without checking, banking on them being empty since the doors looked so dilapidated. When she got to the end of the hall, she took the stairs up. They were a struggle. She was sweating and panting from the exertion.

She concentrated on keeping her legs moving while listening for indications that her captors were close. Her vision started to fade, her thirst was out of control, and she felt cold—all bad signs. She finally reached the next floor and the light was different. It was natural, which meant there had to be windows. Stunned, she saw that it was daylight. *How long have I been here?* She was about to step onto the next level when she heard voices. Her skin crawled; she recognized one of the voices as Number 3. He was moving her way. She had to make a choice: run and hide, or fight. There wasn't much of a choice. Her chances of running away or finding an adequate hiding place were laughable. That left her with option two. If she was going to die, she was going to take these bastards with her.

Elle leaned against the wall and breathed deeply while planning her movements—willing her body to follow the images in her mind. The voices were closing in on her, and she would only have this one chance. She steeled herself and stepped around the corner raising her gun; she fired at the first man she saw. It was the other well-dressed man who had been with 3 earlier. She fired rapidly—two to the body, two to the head—double taps, pure muscle memory. The bullets took him in the chest, and he staggered backward, the two to the head finished him off.

Elle was sighting in on the next man, Number 3, before her first victim fell. She had him, and she fired, but the bodyguard pushed her target out of the way. The bullets hit the big man in the side. The bodyguard turned and pulled his gun, the gunshot wounds he took not even registering in his movements. Elle rapid-fired the rest of her ammunition into the bodyguard to try and put the man down. The advantage was hers in the close quarters since she already had her weapon out, but he still managed to get a shot off at her. Elle felt her left side take a hit, but no pain. She stumbled and fell to one knee, breaking her fall with her broken hand.

The bodyguard was teetering on his feet, blood coming from his chest, mouth, and throat. There was a whistling sound coming from him as he tried to breathe with a hole in his neck, but he hadn't dropped his weapon. The man slowly aimed at her and just as he was about to pull the trigger, she threw herself to the side. The bullet ricocheted off the floor and into the far wall. Elle hit the side wall and lunged back off it. Rolling back toward the bodyguard, she kicked at his knee. There was a snapping sound and the man made a strangled, gurgling cry as he went down.

Elle slammed the butt of her gun into his temple with as much strength as she could muster, and he went slack. She grabbed at his weapon and turned to see Number 3 running away. He had been knocked to the ground when she attacked; and lying there in shock, but when he saw his guard go down, he made a run for it. Elle was dizzy, and her vision was tunneling, but she repeatedly fired at the fleeing man. Her body was revolting against her, and her aim was off, but she thought she saw him stumble before he disappeared out the door at the end of the hall. When the door opened, she saw cars outside. He was getting away.

She used the last of her willpower, to get to her feet, and half-jogged, half-stumbled down the hall. She burst through the door and found several armed men and a fleeing car. The target was getting away, and she was facing multiple gunmen, probably the same mercenaries that had captured her. All the men drew down on her and all she could do was stand there. Elle's vision was completely black along her peripheral and the rest was blurring out of focus. She shook uncontrollably, and her legs buckled. This was it; she was going to make it all this way only to fail. She tried to get up but couldn't. Her legs just wouldn't respond anymore.

Elle pushed herself into a sitting position and tried to have some dignity in her final moments. Looking at the mercenaries in front of her, she raised her head as much as she could and straightened her shoulders. Her vision swam, and felt herself losing her battle with unconsciousness. Elle thought she heard several gunshots. She braced for the impact, at least she wouldn't feel any pain at the end. The impacts didn't come. And it looked like the mercenaries went down. *Am I hallucinating?* Was she in the middle of a firefight? What was happening?

She had a strange feeling like the earth was moving under her, and she fell over. As she was lying on the ground, she saw boots approaching her at a run, and then someone was grabbing her. Her first thought was to fight but she couldn't. Then a face was in front of her. It was Tex. Elle's last thought before everything went black was, *Well, at least I won't die alone.*

CHAPTER 19

Elle was in excruciating pain. Her whole body screamed in protest. Her mind rebelled at the pain and, for one terrifying moment, she was back in that basement, her escape just a figment of her imagination. Panic hit hard, and she wanted to scream, but she held back not wanting them to know she was awake. Elle chanced opening her eyes, but it took a lot of effort. When the light hit, it burned and made her eyes water instantly. She blinked away tears, and tried several times to get her eyes to stay open and focus on her surroundings. She attempted to lift her arms but the pain made it impossible.

Once she was able to focus, she could hardly believe what she saw. It took a while for her heart rate and breathing to slow from her panic attack; and to grasp where she was. She was in a hospital—not a field one, a real one. It was clean and well equipped. Elle could smell the antiseptic quality in the air; and heard the soft electronic sounds of various machines in the room. She was hooked up to several IVs and monitors. She saw bandages and bruises on her arms, and was terrified of what the rest of her looked like.

She looked around the room and was surprised to see that she wasn't alone. Eve was sleeping on the bed next to her. She was fully dressed and lying on top of the covers as if she had just passed out from exhaustion. Elle studied her face. She looked worn, like she hadn't been well. That worried her. What happened? *Did Tex really come for me?* He must have since here she was. But how had he managed that? How long had she been here? What was her condition?

All these thoughts raced in her head; and brought on another wave of panic. Then the door opened, and Jack walked in with two coffees. He didn't see Elle was awake. When he did, it was almost comical. Jack was so startled, he almost dropped the coffees and let out an exclamation of surprise that was so loud, Eve jerked up into a sitting position.

When Eve saw that Elle was awake, she launched off the bed, "Oh, thank God, Elle! I knew you'd be okay." She smiled wider than Elle had ever seen before.

Jack put down the coffees, wiped his hands on his jeans; and joined Eve at Elle's bedside. "How are you feeling? Do you need anything?" he asked.

Elle wasn't sure where to start. "Where am I?" she asked, her voice raspy and course.

"You're at the military hospital in Germany. They evacuated you here after Tex brought you back." Eve answered as she handed her a plastic cup of water with a straw.

Elle took a drink; and tried to get her bearings. Well, that confirmed that she hadn't hallucinated seeing Tex before she blacked out. She wasn't sure how she felt about that. She was grateful to be alive. Tex had saved her, but she never wanted him to risk his life for hers. Elle told him to leave her, made him promise to listen so that he could take care of the team. He'd defied her, but she was alive because of that broken promise.

"How long?" she croaked out.

Eve balked at that. "You've been here for a week now, Elle."

Elle was baffled. A week? How? Why? She was quickly feeling overwhelmed.

Eve must have sensed it, so she continued, "They had you for just under sixteen hours, Elle, and they did a lot of damage. The doctors here had to do multiple surgeries for the gunshot wounds and for the blood clots that were by your spine and at the base of your skull before they moved to your brain or heart. You're lucky to be alive. You lost a lot of blood and took a brutal beating. The doctors said that if it had taken any longer to get you here, you wouldn't have made it. They were shocked that you held on for as long as you did. You're going to need rest and lots of physical therapy. They're guessing six weeks before you'll be able to function normally, but you may never get back to where you were. It's going to take a lot of work. But you've never shied away from that."

Elle didn't want to process what she'd just heard quite yet. Eve was right; she was extremely lucky, but it didn't feel that way at the moment. Elle desperately didn't want to start crying. So, she changed the subject. "What's going on with the rest of the mission? Where's Tex?"

Again, Eve looked uncomfortable.

"Your mission is still active, but Tex got the leadership to delay continuing on with the target list until you recover and can be involved," Jack said. "That's why he's not here. There was a bit of a trade. Tex proposed to lead a small tactical team to make some surgical strikes around Iraq that support our mission. He was able to sell it to the bosses as an interoperability piece."

Before Elle could protest, Jack threw up his hands. "None of us like it, but it was the best way to get them off our backs. Tex chose his team, and Eve and I are here with you until he needs us. His first few ops are going to be pretty straight forward and in direct coordination with the special ops guys we were sharing the compound with. He got the Agency to understand that the support personnel he's targeting now will help our overall mission and keep what we've already done from fading away. And then he played the politics card saying it would earn the Agency some goodwill by showing it can play well with others. Tex intends to keep the internal turmoil going by making certain the Daesh factions stay at war with each other."

Elle fought back her emotional surge. She had no choice but to admit it was a great course of action. Tex could have let them push him to finish the target list on his own, but he was still treating her like his partner—even when she was out of commission. "Who is his team?"

"The shooters from the other op, the ones we grabbed to help pull you out—Julian and Robert. Since they had already been exposed to us, he figured they would be the best option."

"Robert?" Elle asked, fearing she was about to hear a confirmation she didn't want.

"It's Red Shirt's real name, Elle." Eve informed her. She headed off Elle's tirade by putting up a hand and launching into an explanation. "When they took you, Tex hot-wired a car and tracked them from a distance. He thought he lost you a couple of times, and he almost lost his mind. He had me contact the Agency to demand the use of the helo again and to pull together an extraction team. They agreed, and I contacted Julian and Robert to ask them to back Tex to pull you out once we had a location. Julian didn't hesitate but Red Shirt took some convincing. I had to promise him some special recognition from the Agency."

Eve looked repulsed by the memory but continued. "Those animals took you all the way to a tiny little village north of Haditha. When they finally stopped, Tex sent me the location, and we had Julian and Robert flown in on the helo. The daylight hours complicated things, and they had just set up when they saw someone come running out of the building with you right behind him. They watched you run into the security element, and Tex gave the order to take them out. He got you on the helo and had them fly you to Al Asad. He had the base fuel a plane for the medical evacuation to Germany while they were in the air, so that it was ready before the helo even touched down."

"After they got you out, Tex brought Julian and Robert back to the office and made them the offer to work with him as a sort of Special Task Force. Once he got them on board, he asked Jack and me to build him a target list of members of the rival factions that are growing in Daesh. We highlighted the ones that were popular, but not in charge on both sides. He wanted to keep the distrust and instability going until you were back in the game. So, he's targeting the popular guys on both sides to incense the leaders into further infighting."

Elle's anxiety was growing, and she felt sick. But, she couldn't deny that Tex's plan was solid.

Eve continued. "The first few names we gave him were already on the SOF target lists, so they are going to work with the special operations support units for now. Jack and I will link back up with them when they need to go outside what the SOF guys are tracking. Since they have a lot more bureaucracy to deal with when it comes to getting their missions approved, I'm guessing it will be several weeks before they finish working with the SOF support infrastructure. Once they hit that point, it will just be Tex, Julian, and Robert moving forward. Jack and I will be their support."

Eve sat on the corner of Elle's bed and grabbed her hand, trying to be comforting since she could see her increasing distress. "After we secured our stuff in Baghdad, Jack and I flew here and have been keeping constant tabs on you ever since. You were touch and go for a while, but you finally stabilized two days ago. Since then, we've just been waiting for you to wake up."

The monitors started beeping, making sure everyone in the room knew Elle's blood pressure just rose. Her fists clenched so tightly, she heard the splint on her broken fingers crack. The pain she felt now just fueled her anger and determination. It wasn't her team;

they had done admirable work and made the best out of a shitty situation. But Red Shirt was a major problem, and now he was part of their operations. At least Tex had Julian to watch his six until she could get there, but that only bought her a little time. The longer she took, though, the higher the risk to him.

Her eyes blazed as she unclenched her fists. "We've got no time to waste, we've got work to do. The doctors said six weeks of rehab, huh? Fuck that; I'll do it in four. Get the doc. It's time to get back in the game."

ELLE WILL RETURN FOR . . .

THE DEEPER SHADOW

Pulled from the brink of death, Elle Anderson now faces the fight of her life. Physically and emotionally battered, she struggles to recover from the trauma of being captured and tortured by terrorists. How do you win a war being waged in your own mind?

To complicate matters, Elle still has a job to do, and the clock is ticking. If she fails, everybody loses. The terrorist responsible for her capture is still alive and has positioned himself to take over the network.

Her window of opportunity to end him is closing. It's time to get back in the game and finish what she started.

Traveling to Africa, she sets her sights on her target —a charismatic and deadly arms dealer, financier and facilitator of terrorists around the world. To beat him, she must immerse herself in his world.

When tested, will Elle remember whose side she's on?

TURN THE PAGE FOR A SNEAK PEEK OF BOOK 2 . . .

THE DEEPER SHADOW
AN ELLE ANDERSON NOVEL
BOOK 2 OF 3

A creak was the only warning she got. She jumped to the side of the door just as it flung open. Red Shirt had Eve by the throat and was using her as a shield. Elle barely registered that Eve's pajamas had been torn to expose her breasts, or that she was sobbing. Elle darted in low, just out of Red Shirt's eyeline and drove the blade of her knife into the exposed portion of his thigh. And then she twisted.

He wailed in agony and lost his grip on Eve.

Elle pulled her out of Red Shirt's reach. "Run, get out of here," she commanded.

"What about you?"

"Go, Eve! Now!"

Elle didn't turn to make sure that Eve had listened but thought she heard the faint sound of gravel crushing, a sign that Eve was running. This was going to end here. Red Shirt had crossed the line and he was going to pay, consequences be damned.

She watched as he wrenched the blade from his flesh. He was grinning. It was all bravado, as she knew the blood loss would weaken him and slow him down. But now he had her knife and she was unarmed.

"Just you and me, bitch. You're going to learn your place."

Elle didn't respond. She wasn't going to play his game.

He was going to play hers....

ACKNOWLEDGMENTS

It's impossible to overstate the gratitude I have for all those who have supported me through this endeavor. Foremost is everyone who I am fortunate enough to call family; whether through blood, military service, or close personal ties, you mean the world to me. Particularly Jake, Sierra, Lindsey, Marcia, Chrissy, Erika, and Street, love you guys. Also, thank you to Ken Atchity and Lisa Cerasoli for taking a chance on me, and for all your guidance and support.

TO MY READERS

I hope you enjoyed reading this novel. Your feedback is important to me, so please consider leaving a review for *Shadow Game* on Amazon.com.

SHADOW
GAME

Made in the USA
Middletown, DE
24 September 2020